# ANDROMEDA

## ROMANCING A GOD

### CHARLEY MARSH

TIMBERDOODLE PRESS

Andromeda

Copyright © 2019 by Charley Marsh

All rights reserved.

Published 2019 by Timberdoodle Press LLC.

*Andromeda* is a work of fiction. The characters, incidents, and places are the product of the author's imagination or are used fictitiously. Any resemblance to actual events, locales, or persons living or dead is entirely coincidental.

No part of this book may be reproduced in any form or by any electronic or mechanical means, including information storage and retrieval systems, without written permission from the author, except for the use of brief quotations in a book review. For more information contact the publisher: https://www.timberdoodlepress.com/

All rights reserved

Print Book ISBN# 978-1-945856-66-2

Cover Art: ooGleb/depositphotos.com

# INTRODUCTION

Andromeda's Story

Andromeda was the daughter of King Cepheus and Queen Cassiopeia. Yep, another beautiful princess. Unfortunately for Andromeda her arrogant mother bragged about her daughter's beauty, claiming that Andromeda was more beautiful than the Nereids (sea nymphs) which understandably angered the nymphs. No woman likes having another woman's beauty thrown in her face.

Poseidon got involved and sent a sea monster to destroy Cepheus' kingdom. A little over the top as far as punishment goes but we're talking about the gods here. They don't do anything in a small, understated way.

In order to save the kingdom Cepheus was forced to sacrifice Andromeda to the sea monster by chaining her to a rock so she could be eaten. Our hero Perseus flew by on the winged Pegasus, fell in love with the beautiful princess and . . . you'll have to read on to learn how it all works out in a modern day romance.

# CHAPTER 1

ANDROMEDA WHITE STARED BLINDLY at the spreadsheet numbers on her screen and sighed. It was nearly six on a Friday night. Yet another Friday evening that saw her toiling alone on the seventh floor of the Cepheus White Building while her co-workers headed off to have drinks with friends or home to share dinner with waiting families.

Not that she could have gone with them even if someone had thought to invite her. Tonight she had to attend yet another stuffy event with her parents.

The Cepheus White Sports gala was always held the third Friday evening in June and that meant that tonight she had to paste on a smile and make friendly with people she mostly saw only once a year–at the gala–as well as total strangers. Never an easy thing for someone who tripped over her own tongue with shyness.

Whoever had decreed these modern business-social affairs as worthy of the term "gala" had been way off base. Gala came from the French "gale" which meant rejoice. As far as Andi could tell there was no rejoicing at these events, only elbow rubbing and too many people trying to impress one another.

Unfortunately they also tried to impress her because they thought she'd put in a good word for them with her father. Which meant she'd be forced to talk when she'd much rather stand quietly off to the side and observe. She'd learned at an early age that people who were nice to her usually wanted something.

She scowled at the dress bag hanging on the back of her office door. It had arrived several hours ago by special courier, along with a note from her mother informing Andi that she had just the earrings and necklace to go with it and her parents would pick her up at her condo at seven-thirty.

The knowledge that she would once again be paraded in front of people like a prized bull settled like a stone around Andi's heart.

She closed the spreadsheet, shut down her computer, and leaned back in her chair to ponder her life. Her office was small and had no window and was a step up from the rows of gray-blue cubicles that filled the large space outside her door. Gray carpet covered the floor. Two hard-backed oak chairs and her desk, a large gray metal affair with zero personality and not a smidgeon of beauty, filled the space.

She'd rather have a cubicle if it meant a few of the other workers would accept her. Invite her to have an after work drink with them. Or share a pizza. She liked pizza a lot. She certainly preferred it to the fancy tidbits she'd be served at the gala.

Andi stretched her long body with a heavy sigh. Maybe this one would be different. Maybe the servers would offer trays of pizza bites. She smiled at the thought. Her mother would consider such fare "common" and not suitably impressive. She loved her mother but the woman was an undeniable snob.

Her co-workers would think she was nuts to prefer a glass of wine in a bar with friends over a fancy dress gala event. Maybe they'd be right. Maybe she had been spoiled by too many business social affairs. Her parents started dragging her to them when she turned sixteen in the hopes that she'd develop the relationships necessary to take over Cepheus White Sports when her father retired.

She supposed the first time she'd attended an event with her parents she must have been awed and excited. She couldn't remember. Eight years had passed since that first event and there'd been too many since. The people were always the same, the conversations about nothing.

All but one row of lights snapped off outside her office door. The night watchman was making his rounds. He knew that Andi was always the last to leave, especially at the end of the work week and he left a row of lights on to guide her out. She heard the elevator ding as the watchman headed back down and knew she needed to leave, but remained seated.

She had argued against working for her father but he had sabotaged any attempt she made at finding a job that she wanted to do. She'd finally given up after being turned down for every position she'd applied for, even entry level positions for the simplest of jobs. Her father, Cepheus White, founder and president of Cepheus White Sports, carried a lot of clout.

Andi slipped off her heels and pulled on her running shoes, bagging each heel separately as her mother had trained her and placed them in her leather tote bag.

Her mother would have a fit if she saw her only daughter wearing black and red sneakers with a sage green linen suit.

The thought made Andi smile. Her mother Cass was a true believer in always looking your best under any circumstances. Andi had bought the ugly running shoes on a whim, probably to defy her mother although she hadn't considered that at the time.

She looked around her sparsely furnished office with a nagging sense of disgust. While her mother had never worked–inside nor outside the White home–Andi needed to work. Was it too much to ask that the work be useful and make her feel that she was making the world better in some small way?

Running numbers for the marketing department on the floor above wasn't Andi's idea of making the world a better place. Her father had wanted to start her in a large corner office on the eighth floor but she had dug in her heels and refused. At least she'd won that skirmish, although she'd have preferred to work in a cubicle and not be singled out.

The seventh floor cubicles housed the Cepheus White Sports customer service department, the guys and gals who took the phone orders and also keyed in orders from the company's extensive website. Andi tallied the number of daily orders taken for the various product lines and sent them to the sales reps on the eighth floor so they knew what to order more of and what wasn't selling.

It had taken less than half a day for the word to get around that she was the owner's daughter and any hope she had of making a few real friends who would like her for herself had died.

Andi shook off the old thoughts. It was time to head back to her condo to dress. Her parents would both fuss and lecture her on the importance of punctuality if she kept them waiting even a few minutes.

She snapped off her lights, pulled the dress bag from the hook on the door and hung it over her arm, picked up her leather tote, and closed and locked her office.

The center row of lights didn't quite reach the outer edges of the broad cubicle space but she wasn't afraid of the shadows. She had learned that shadows were her friend. A shy woman could melt into the background if she had shadows to hide in.

Her running shoes made no noise on the carpet. The single row of florescent lights buzzed faintly overhead. She could smell the remains of someone's curry lunch and too many varieties of perfume on the air.

Andi had never cared for perfume. In her opinion women tended to overspray. Perfumes made her sinuses swell and always seemed too artificial to her.

She understood why men and women wore heavy scents during England's Georgian era. Or was that the Edwardian era? Bathing was a rare occurrence during both of those eras and people splashed on heavy scents to hide their body odor. These days there was no excuse for not bathing unless you were homeless or too ill.

She slapped the last light switches down as she went out the stairwell door. The seventh floor of the Cepheus White building went dark behind her. The heavy fire door closed with a soft click and she was alone in the dim concrete stairwell. She began to run down the steps, her shoes making a soft shuffle on the smooth cement.

She counted the steps off as she went, a habit she had started and couldn't seem to drop. She counted them on the way up in the morning and again on the way down at the end of the day.

She never took the elevator, preferring to use the stairs

for the exercise. She sat around too much during the day as it was, glued to a computer screen until black squiggles and lines danced in front of her eyes. She had never wanted to be a computer geek. It came easy to her–most intellectual things did–but that didn't mean she enjoyed it.

One hundred and eighty two steps brought her to the ground floor of her father's building where she exited the stairwell into the lobby.

"Good night, Gus." She waved to the night watchman.

"Good night, Miss Andromeda. I hope you have a date for tonight."

"Just with my parents, Gus. You know how it is. You're taken and I can't find anyone else to measure up." Gus's wrinkled face lit up with pleasure.

"Ahhh, Miss Andromeda. If only we'd met when I was a young man. I'd have swept you off your feet like you deserve. You have a good weekend now."

Andi stepped out into a mild spring evening. Turning left, she headed toward her riverside condo at a brisk pace, weaving in and out of knots of noisy college students and tourists heading for the many bars and restaurants in La Crosse's historic district.

She loved this section of the busy college town. Loved the fancy old brick buildings that had been built in response to several fires that had leveled the young city more than a century before. Modern store fronts now filled many of their ground floors but the upper floors, many made into apartments, retained their original bay windows and the intricate brickwork on the upper floors delighted her.

She turned down State Street and immediately cut through an alley that would take her to Main. The alley was wide enough for a single car to pass through and was remarkably clean even with the dumpsters for the burger pub and credit union that backed onto it. Most of La Crosse's alleys were clean and tended. It was one of the many reasons she loved it.

Andi was nearing the pub's dumpster when she spied the brown paper bag, a grocery store bag with the top folded over, set on top of a pile of green trash bags filling the pub's dumpster. The paper bag rattled and shook as she neared, making her pulse jump. Then it was still.

Suspecting that the bag was a college punk's idea of a prank, she looked up and down the alley to see if anyone was watching her but she was the only one there. She took a step closer to the bag and it shook again. The unpleasant stench of rotting garbage and wet cardboard filled her nose.

She didn't have time for pranks. She barely had time for a shower if she was going to meet her parents on time. She turned away from the bag and it gave out a pitiful mew. Whirling back, Andi picked up the bag and carefully unfolded the top. A very angry kitten mewed up at her and leaped for the opening.

"Oh you poor thing," Andi crooned. She set down her tote and scooped inside the bag, wincing as the kitten's tiny claws dug into her wrist. It stared at her with wide golden eyes. It had calico fur, more black than orange or white, and it was spitting mad. It hissed at Andi to show its displeasure.

"I don't blame you, little one. What a rotten thing to do to a helpless animal." Obviously the kitten's callous owner had decided they didn't want her and had tossed her into the dumpster knowing full well it would be crushed in the garage truck's compressor.

"Well, I can't leave you here. You'll have to come home with me until I can take you to the shelter on Monday." She held the kitten against her chest and leaned down to grab her tote. Fortunately she only had a few more blocks to walk.

The kitten would need food. And a litter box. She could feed it a can of tuna tonight but the litter box was a problem.

CHAPTER 2

By the time Andi let herself into her condo the kitten was snuggled under her neck and purring and she had figured out that it could stay in her bathtub until after the gala. She'd head to the nearest Wally World for cat supplies after she got home and changed her clothes. She could donate whatever she bought to the shelter when she dropped off the kitten.

Digging her keys out of her tote to open her door was a bit of a struggle with both hands full, but eventually Andi made it inside her condo. The kitten clung to her neck with her curved needle claws, mewing her displeasure at being disturbed from her nap.

Andi kicked the door shut behind her, dropped the tote in the entry hall, and hung the dress bag on the row of hooks to the left of the door before attempting to soothe the upset animal.

"You have to work with me here," she told the kitten, holding it up in both hands so they were eye to eye. Two golden eyes blinked at her and the kitten mewed loudly.

"You're probably hungry. I can feel your little ribs. Let's

9

get you something to eat and drink while I shower. I don't drink milk so you'll have to settle for water."

Andi walked through the large living room toward the open kitchen area in the back. Floor to ceiling multi-paned windows made up the entire south wall of her condo, filling her space with light. The old oak floors had been refinished and glowed honey-brown in the waning light.

Originally a button factory, the three story brick building housed six condos, two to a floor. Andi's was on the top floor, south side. The building had escaped the wrecking ball when the riverfront underwent its most recent redevelopment phase. A smart and savvy developer, recognizing the latest craze for warehouses-turned-condos, snapped up the building while others less fortunate fell.

She loved her spacious one bedroom condo, partly because she had saved the money for the down payment without any help from her father, but mostly because of the space itself.

The wall of south-facing windows looked down the Mississippi River alive with pleasure boats and moored houseboats and massive river barges guided by large tugboats. There was always something going on once the ice melted away and she loved to sit and watch the river traffic.

Further down, the two large blue bridges crossing from wooded Pettibone Island to La Crosse arced high over the water.

She didn't have time to enjoy the view tonight however. She checked the time and set the kitten on the kitchen floor. It immediately tried to chase after her, its claws scrabbling for purchase on the bare wood planks.

"Patience, little one. I'm getting you something to eat as fast as I can." Andi dumped a can of tuna onto one of her sand colored pottery plates and set it beside the kitten. The hungry animal wasted no time. It climbed onto the plate and began to devour the tuna.

Andi's stomach growled. "I wish I was dining with you. I'm so not a fan of catered finger food," she told the kitten. "It's too difficult to hold a drink and napkin and eat at the same time. Or at least I haven't managed to learn the trick."

It felt strange to have someone to talk to in her condo. Other than her mother occasionally dropping by no one had ever visited her.

Ordinarily she'd make herself something to eat before the gala and ignore the finger food, something she'd recently begun to do, but she'd delayed too long leaving the office. She'd have to skip washing her hair as it was. Her long hair was so thick it took forever to dry even with a blowdryer.

Andi showered quickly, pulled her hair back into a chignon, and pulled on her favorite soft terry robe. She applied only the barest of makeup—her mother had given specific instructions to go with the dress she'd had delivered to the office.

Andi always listened to her mother when it came to makeup, especially when she hadn't seen the dress she was to wear. Cass made a religion out of looking her absolute best and always had spot-on suggestions for her only daughter.

A light touch with soft bronze and champagne eyeshadows, a little tinted gloss on her full lips, and a quick brush of bronze-tinted blusher and she was done. She checked on the kitten on her way back to the entry to grab the dress bag.

The kitten had curled up into a tiny ball beside the mostly empty plate and appeared to be fast asleep. She leaned down and ran a finger gently over its back, feeling each knobby bump of its spine. "Poor thing. What kind of monster would throw a live animal into the trash?"

The kitchen clock caught Andi's eye and she groaned. She

only had ten minutes left to dress. She flew down the hall, grabbed the dress bag and flew back to her bedroom. She laid the long bag on her bed and yanked open the zipper.

"What's this?" She held up a silky waterfall of deep navy. At least it had nice wide shoulder straps. The last dress her mother had sent her had been a strapless affair and Andi had spent the entire evening either tugging on its neckline or clamping her elbows to her sides so the dress wouldn't creep down.

She turned the dress to look for the back zipper and yelped. There was no zipper. There wasn't even a back. "Jeezus Mother, what were you thinking?"

She had no time to hunt up an alternative outfit now. She took off her bra and slid into the dress, careful not to muss her hair or makeup.

At least the front was modest, she thought as she checked her image in the full length bedroom mirror. The built in bra supported her breasts well enough. She liked the high neckline that skimmed her collarbones and the dress hugged her curves in a flattering fashion.

She took a step back toward the bed and most of her right thigh slid free of the dress.

For a brief moment Andi considered tossing the dress and wearing one of her work suits to the gala–but only for a brief moment. She had been raised to be a dutiful daughter and she knew these social engagements were important to her father's business.

Still, she was going to have a serious discussion with her mother about what was and wasn't acceptable apparel.

She pulled on the silver stiletto heels her mother had packed with the dress and checked herself again in the mirror. She was going to have to have another talk with Mother about buying her five inch heels as well. At five eleven she already towered over most people. Adding five inches to her height made her feel like a circus freak.

Andi sighed and consigned herself to another uncomfortable evening looking down on people. She grabbed the kitten, water, and tuna remains, and placed them in the bath tub.

"I shouldn't be too late. I'm really sorry but I can't leave you to wander the condo unsupervised."

The kitten looked up at her and gave a pitiful mew.

"Yeah, well I'm not happy about a lot of things either. We'll talk about it when I get home." She grabbed a towel and made a nest in one end of the tub and placed the kitten on it. She felt better when she saw it begin to knead the thick terry towel with its tiny paws.

"I'll be home as soon as I can. Now if I can just get through the next few hours in this excuse for a dress. Wish me luck." Andi grabbed the small silver beaded clutch her mother had bagged with the dress and shoes and ran out the door at seven-thirty on the dot.

Her father's big, black customized Mercedes was already waiting at the front door as she knew it would be. She'd never known her father to be late for anything.

"Hi, Charles." Andi greeted the driver with a big smile and an affectionate kiss on the cheek. Charles had been with her father for as long as she could remember and she looked on him as an honorary member of the family. It had been Charles who had taught her how to ride a bike during a brief summer visit home. Charles who greeted her at the airport when she had come home for holiday visits. Charles who sent her weekly emails keeping her abreast of happenings at home.

She realized with a start that she felt closer to her father's driver than she did to her parents. How sad was that?

Charles's blue eyes sparkled at her as he opened the rear door of the car. "Good evening, Miss Andi. You're looking very fine tonight."

"Thank you, Charles. I blame my mother for that." Andi grinned, gathered the slim skirt of her dress around her, and slid into the car as gracefully as possible.

"There you are, Andromeda. Your father was sure you'd be late. You didn't leave the office until after six. Here. Put these on." Cass White unrolled a silk lined jewelry roll and placed a pair of earrings in Andi's hand.

She should have known that her mother would call Gus to make sure she didn't work too late, Andi thought with a sigh as she put on the earrings. Each earring had three long strands of diamonds set in platinum that fell nearly to her shoulders and was probably worth a small fortune. Her mother didn't believe in paste.

Cass looked at her daughter with a critical eye and nodded. "They'll do. You were smart to wear your hair up. I forgot to tell you to do that." She held out a long chain of diamonds and Andi leaned forward for her mother to clasp it around her neck. Cass adjusted the long strand of diamonds until they hung down the center of her bare back.

Andi twitched as the cold jewels hit her bare skin. "They feel weird on my back, Mother. Do I have to wear the necklace? The earrings are stunning enough."

"You'll get used to the feel. By the end of the evening you won't even know they're there. That dress demands something extra special."

"About this dress–"

"No time to talk wardrobe, ladies." Cepheus White sat in the seat opposite with a small glass of bourbon in his hand. The Mercedes SUV had been reconfigured on the inside to resemble a stretch limo without all of the stretch but with several of the amenities like a small bar and facing seats.

"I need you to chat up a few of the businessmen who will be there tonight, Andi."

Andi groaned. "You know I hate that, Dad. Why can't Mother do it? She's so much better than I am at that sort of thing."

"Normally I'd agree, but these are up and comers, closer to your age than your mother's. I want them to see that Cepheus White Sports is young and hip and keeping with the times. You'll impress them."

This time Andi grimaced. "'Hip' went out decades ago, Dad, and I'm not so sure I'll be able to impress them. You know how tongue-tied I get around strangers. They usually end up thinking I'm an idiot."

"You'll be fine," her mother said firmly. "You just need more practice, that's all. Tonight you'll get some. Just remember to get them talking about themselves. Usually a question or two is all it takes. Then you simply listen and smile as if they're the most fascinating person in the room."

"I wouldn't be too sure about the 'I'll be fine' part," Andi muttered under her breath. She sat on the edge of the seat, not wanting to feel the leather against her bare back. Why hadn't she grabbed a stole to cover herself with? Of course. She hadn't thought of it because she'd been rushing out the door. Now she would pay for staying at the office too long.

"Here we are," Cepheus said unnecessarily, as Charles stopped in front of the historic and upscale Washburn Hotel, another renovation project in La Crosse's historic district. The brick hotel, set in a converted late 1800s candy factory, was fast becoming a favorite destination spot for travelers passing through La Crosse.

Well-dressed men and women poured through the hotel's

front entry. It looked like the tickets for the gala had sold well which meant the evening would be a squeeze. At least it was taking place on the hotel's rooftop terrace. She'd be able to get much needed air, unlike at most of her parents' affairs.

"Here we go, ladies." Charles held the door open and extended a hand toward Andi. "Looks like a good crowd, Miss Andi."

"Sadist." Andi glared at Charles when he turned to help her mother. Charles knew how much she hated large groups of people.

"Bring the car around at eleven, Charles. If we're going to be any later I'll call you." Cepheus White tucked his wife's hand into his elbow and offered his other arm to his daughter. "Remember to smile, Andi."

Andi pasted a smile on her face and took her father's arm.

# CHAPTER 3

"I THOUGHT you said this was going to be a small affair. I can barely breathe." Percy jabbed his half-brother Zee in the ribs. "You know I hate this kind of thing."

"Are you whining, Perce?"

"No, of course not. Real men don't whine. I'm flat out complaining. Why did you drag me here tonight?"

Both men had inherited their father's tall, muscular frame and classic features–broad foreheads, full, sensuous mouths, strong noses and jaws. Only their hair and eyes differed. Unlike Zee's current cap of short black hair, Percy wore his thick, chestnut brown locks tied back in a queue. His eyes were a smoky moss green instead of gray. Neither man had any trouble attracting women although Zee was now happily married.

"You could have stayed at the house and looked after the kids." Zee's wife Pandora gave Percy a mischievous smile. "They do love their uncles."

Percy pointed a finger at her. "Last time I babysat for you I ended up having to clean the kitchen from top to bottom.

You neglected to warn me that baking cookies with three children under the age of six might not be a good idea."

"My kitchen sparkled after. I was ever so grateful." Pandora's smile widened.

"Yeah, right." But Percy found himself smiling at his sister in law. He'd had fun with his nephews and niece even if it had taken him hours to clean up afterward.

He looked over the crowd filling the hotel's roof terrace. Several women gave him appraising glances as they caught his eye but he ignored their silent invitations to join them.

Percy wasn't looking to hook up during this visit to check up on his brother. The plan was to stop overnight in La Crosse, check out Zee's new business venture, and then head back out tomorrow afternoon.

Unfortunately Zee and Pandora had already made plans to attend the gala and had dragged him along. Since the gala was sponsored by someone connected to Zee's new venture Percy had agreed to accompany them. Now, in spite of what he'd said to Pandora about babysitting he wished he'd stayed home with the kids.

The warm summer evening had brought out a lot of bared shoulders and legs. Nice shoulders and legs for the most part. He knew that the tickets for the gala hadn't been cheap. Wealthy men tended to collect attractive wives and have pretty daughters. He acknowledged that it might not be a politically correct assessment but it was a fact of life in the social circle most of the gala guests ran in.

He needed to move around. He was beginning to feel rooted to that particular spot near the edge of the terrace.

"Want another beer, Zee? What are you drinking, Pan?" Percy took their drink orders and began working his way through the crowd toward the bar. Several women stopped him with a hand to his arm and introduced themselves. He responded politely and made his getaway as quickly as possible.

He had just stepped inside the terrace bar and was waiting patiently in line to order the drinks when he heard the elevator ding. He looked over his shoulder and watched with idle curiosity as an older man with thick black hair shot through with silver exited the cage with an elegantly dressed, beautiful woman on his arm. Someone near him whispered that Cepheus White had just arrived.

So that was Cepheus White. Percy knew about Cepheus White's sports memorabilia company through Zee. His brother was considering authorizing Cepheus's company to sell an exclusive line of products sporting images and symbols of the Olympic gods.

He studied the head of Cepheus White Sports as Cepheus and his wife were instantly surrounded. The couple smiled and shook hands and appeared genuinely happy to be there.

Behind them the elevator door began to close. A hand shot out and the door opened again. Percy watched, curious now, to see who had ridden up with the Whites but was so slow to exit the elevator. The door began to slide closed again.

This time an entire woman shot out of the elevator before the door closed completely. She nearly lost her balance but righted herself before falling.

Percy caught his breath and felt his abs tighten. He had never before seen such a beautiful woman. She would stand out for her beauty even among the goddesses. He stood rooted to the floor, unable to take his gaze off her.

The woman stood in front of the closed elevator, taller than all of the women and many of the men on the rooftop, the epitome of elegance and beauty.

She slowly scanned the room, her face expressionless. Her eyes passed over Percy. Shot back.

It pleased him to see a slight flush rise to her impassive face. He stared at the woman until she lowered her eyes. Mr. and Mrs. White turned and spoke to her and she joined their group as they moved deeper into the terrace crowd.

Percy made it to the bar and ordered the drinks, then managed to carry them through the press of bodies back to Zee and Pandora without spilling or sloshing on anyone. He handed them out and took a long pull on his own beer.

There were some good craft beer brewers in the American midwest and he always enjoyed sampling something different. This one was an India Pale Ale, a little too citrusy for his taste, but fresh and cold.

While he drank he scanned the room for the blonde from the elevator. She wasn't hard to spot. She stood on the opposite side of the open terrace, at least a full head taller than any other woman there. He liked the way she kept her shoulders squared and didn't slouch in a vain attempt to hide her superior height. It showed self-confidence, something he genuinely admired in others.

The woman's blond hair was pulled into some kind of knot high on the back of her head and her ears dripped diamonds. Probably paste, he thought. There was a diamond choker around her slender neck as well. The dress showed off well-toned arms and shoulders and a slim yet curvy figure. Her eyes were long and dark and capped with pale, arched eyebrows, her mouth full.

While he watched her, an older man joined the woman's group and she turned to greet him. Percy nearly spit out his beer when he saw her naked back. The dress plunged all the way to the curve of a lush ass. A single strand of diamonds hung between her shoulder blades to her narrow waist.

This was a woman who knew she had a fine body and didn't mind showing it off.

"Wow."

"What?" Zee turned around. "Oh. That's Cepheus White's daughter. First time I've seen her in person. Her picture's always in the weekend society pages. She's even better looking than her photos."

His wife elbowed him in the ribs.

"Ow. Between you and Perce I'm going to be bruised tomorrow." Zee kissed the tip of Pandora's nose. "You're even prettier, sweetheart. You know I have eyes for no one but you."

It was the truth, Percy knew. Zee had been a busy playboy before he met Pandora, but once they met no other woman interested him.

"My friend Maggie works with the daughter," Pandora offered. "She says Andromeda is really cold and stuck up."

"Andromeda? That's an unusual name." Percy watched Andromeda smile. "She's talking to people. She can't be that stuck up."

"Maggie says they call her the ice queen. She never talks to any of the customer service reps even though they work on the same floor."

"Ice queen, huh?" Percy remembered the blush he'd seen rise to Andromeda's cheeks when she realized he was staring at her. No ice queen would blush that easily. Curiosity aroused, he turned to Zee.

"Introduce me."

"I can't. I've never met her."

Percy frowned at his brother. "You know her father, right? You can introduce me."

"I know Cepheus, yes. Never met the daughter though."

Percy nudged his arm. "Doesn't matter. Introduce me to the old man and I'll handle it from there."

Zee pursed his lips. "I don't want you to queer the deal I'm working with Cepheus. A lot of family members are depending on me to fill the coffers that support us all."

Percy merely stared at him.

Zee sighed."Sure. I can introduce you, but if you mess up this deal I'm telling Father it was all your fault."

Since Percy had only recently met the father they shared the threat meant little to him.

"Hold my beer please, honey. I won't be but a minute." Zee handed his wife his beer and headed toward Cepheus White's group but when they got there it wasn't as easy as he had anticipated. It seemed everyone at the gala wanted to speak with White. They stood three and four deep around the man.

"Never mind," Percy said into his ear. "Go back to Pan. I'll manage."

Zee instantly deserted him.

Percy settled on the edge of the crowd where he could watch Andromeda's face. She listened attentively when anyone spoke to her and responded when asked a question. She even smiled occasionally, but he noticed that she never initiated conversation and her smiles never reached her eyes.

She held a small silver beaded clutch in her left hand, a glass of white wine in her right. He never saw her sip the drink. Interesting. Was the wine a prop? She was there and definitely getting a lot of looks from the men around her, but she didn't seem to be part of the gala. More of an observer than a participant.

His curiosity about the famed ice queen grew. She either felt she was above the crowd in status or she was bored with the whole thing. He worked his way closer, snagging a couple of miniature mushroom tarts as a server walked by. He washed them down with a swallow of his beer, grimacing at the clash of the too citrusy IPA and the mushrooms.

The corners of Andi's lips curved up slightly. She looked away as soon as she realized he'd caught her watching him.

"Andromeda, darling. I was hoping you'd be here tonight." A familiar looking man kissed both her cheeks.

"André. It's so nice to see you. I didn't realize you were in town." This time the smile that lit her face reached her eyes, giving Percy a small twinge of jealousy.

Ah. No wonder the man looked familiar. Percy hadn't recognized international soccer star André Lightfoot out of uniform. The famous athlete wore black dress pants and a suit jacket with the sleeves pushed up over a black tee shirt. Was that the new casual-chic look?

Whatever it was called the look suited the handsome athlete, and judging from the women openly staring at André they thought so as well.

André said something to the Ice Queen that made her laugh—a warm, husky sound that made Perseus even more curious about her—then André kissed her cheeks again and moved off.

Perseus took another step closer but before he could speak to her another handsome man, this one with carefully coiffed blonde hair, pushed his way through the crowd and came between them.

Perseus hung back and watched.

The man ran a possessive, tanned hand down Andromeda's naked back. She stiffened in response and stepped away from the hand, exposing a long length of slim, toned thigh through a slit in the skirt of the dress.

She certainly didn't dress like an ice queen. That dress was temptation in silk.

Perseus took a step closer in case she needed someone to run interference for her.

"Andi, sweetheart, you look absolutely *divine* in that dress. Your mother sure knows how to pick them." The man chuckled and stroked her arm.

Percy watched Andromeda's jaw tighten. He'd seen enough. The bozo with the wandering hands had to go. He moved closer and was again about to speak when Andromeda caught someone's eye and gave the slightest of nods.

A quick glance to his side told him that Cepheus White had just signaled his daughter. Interesting. He remained where he was, held his tongue and waited to see what it was all about.

"Angus, what a pleasure to see you again."

Her voice made him think of warm maple syrup dripping over a stack fluffy silver dollar pancakes. Smooth and sweet and throaty. It sent a pleasant shiver up Percy's spine. From where he stood he could see that her eyes were the deepest blue he'd ever seen and they matched her dress.

He could also see that the smile she gave Angus didn't reach her eyes. Apparently Angus was not as favored as André had been.

"The pleasure is all mine, Andi, I assure you. You're the most beautiful woman here you know."

Percy had to give Angus points for stating the obvious. Andromeda White was definitely the most beautiful woman at the gala.

"I'm only in town for two nights. Andi."

Angus had lowered his voice but Percy stood close enough to hear the words.

"I'm hoping we can get together. We seem to have missed

each other my last trip. I believe we have things–important things–to . . . *discuss.*"

The leer in Angus's voice was unmistakable. Percy took another sip of beer while he waited to hear how Andromeda would handle the arrogant ass. The movement of the bottle caught her eye. She looked at him over Angus's hair. For a brief second he saw a bleak resignation in her expression, and then she lowered her eyes to her companion.

She needed help. She didn't want to see this Angus bozo no matter what her father demanded of her. It was time to move in.

Percy looked for a place to set his empty bottle. He settled on a passing tray but when he turned back he saw that Cepheus White had joined his daughter and the grabby bozo.

"Glad you could make it, Angus," Cepheus told him, clapping a hand on the other man's shoulder. "I trust Andi is treating you right?"

"Not yet, Cepheus, but she will." Angus smiled the smile of a hungry wolf. "We were just about to make dinner plans for tomorrow night. Isn't that right, Andi?"

Perseus bristled at the smug certainty in Angus's voice. He looked at Andromeda. Her face was an unreadable mask but her fingertips had gone white on her beaded clutch.

"Glad to hear it. I'm sure my daughter will treat you right. If you'd like to join me at the club in the morning, Angus, I'm putting together a foursome. I'd like to run some new projects by you that I think you'll be interested in."

Perseus wasn't sure what propelled him forward but he suspected it was the idea of Cepheus White essentially pimping out his daughter to a plastic lecher like Angus.

He put a wide smile on his face and stepped into the tight group, maneuvering his body between Angus and Andi.

"There you are, Andi. Sorry, you know how my brother

can talk. I couldn't get away." He turned to Andromeda's father and held out his hand. "You must be Cepheus White. I'm Perseus, Zee's brother. Zee tells me he's thinking of working a business deal with you."

Perseus didn't have to spell it out for the old man. He could see instant understanding in Cepheus's eyes. As Zee's brother he'd better be treated right.

"You know this man, Andi?" Anger tightened Angus's voice. He obviously didn't like the interruption.

Good.

Perseus held out his hand while looking down his nose at the arrogant ass. He had a good five inches on the man and wasn't shy about using his height advantage.

"Name's Perseus. I couldn't help overhearing you say you were planning to take Andi here to dinner tomorrow night. I'm afraid that won't be possible as she's already agreed to have dinner with me and I'm not about to let her back out. Isn't that right, Andi?"

Angus's face flushed with anger beneath his too smooth tan. His lips thinned into a hard, angry line.

Cepheus looked at his daughter in surprise. "You have a date and didn't tell your mother?"

Andi quickly hid her shocked embarrassment. Even if it was true—and it was—did her father have to make it sound like she never went out on dates? Or that she told her mother everything? She wanted to throttle him for being so gauche.

She had no idea who Perseus was. She'd noticed him watching her when she'd made her less than elegant exit from the elevator, and had noticed him again when he grimaced from the combination of finger food and beer.

Assuming he was one of the sports figures her father often invited to his business parties she had been getting up the nerve to speak with him when Angus had waylaid her.

If he wasn't a sports figure then who was he?

Whoever he was he'd just given her an out. She had learned from her one and only dinner with Angus that dinner involved a lot of her dodging the older man's wandering, grabby hands.

"I-I guess I forgot to tell Mother." She took a deep breath and turned to Angus. "I'm so sorry, Angus, but I *am* busy tomorrow. Maybe your next trip to town."

She despised Angus Ames but knew that he was an important supplier for her father's company. Her father had told her to be extra nice to him. She suspected that Angus was looking for a whole lot more nice than she was willing to give but she couldn't talk to her father about that. It would embarrass both of them.

Perseus smiled at her and something fluttered in her stomach.

"Hmmph. I may not be in the mood to ask next time." Angus gave a curt nod to Cepheus and stalked off.

"I'd better go smooth some ruffled feathers." Cepheus sighed. He gave his daughter an exasperated look and took off after Angus. Everyone else drifted away from Andi now that she was persona non grata.

Perseus smiled at her. "That went well."

# CHAPTER 4

ANDI DIDN'T KNOW how to react to the handsome, arrogant man who stood before her. He had rescued her from dinner with Angus Ames, a man she detested, but he couldn't possibly expect her to have dinner with him. He was a complete stranger. Besides, if he was one of her father's clients then he was yet another person wanting to use her to curry favor with her father.

She gave him her coldest, most distant look. A look guaranteed to make anyone slink off. And realized he was watching her, his green eyes filled with amusement and intelligence. In her heels they stood eye to eye which made him six four. She blinked and swallowed.

A tall, well built, compelling stranger, but a stranger nonetheless.

She should probably say something.

"I-I guess I should thank you," was all she could manage. His eyes were a really pretty green and there was a slight curl to his dark brown hair. He wore it shoulder length and tied back and she wondered how it would look loose.

Women probably fawned all over him. Well, she wouldn't

be one of them. She was above that. Or maybe not above it, she simply knew better than to get involved with one of her father's clients. Been there, done that, not going there again.

Percy could feel Andromeda withdrawing now that they were alone. He wasn't about to let her slip away. He stuck out his hand and took the glass of wine from her so he could clasp her now free hand in his.

"There's no need for you to thank me. My name is Perseus," he told her. "Most people call me Percy. I would very much like to take you to dinner tomorrow night. Will you let me?"

His voice was deep and smooth and quiet and it sent a small thrill down her naked back. His eyes were still amused but also serious.

"I don't know. I don't know you." Oh, she *wanted* to go to dinner with this handsome stranger but she knew better. History had taught her that men only hit on Andromeda White for two reasons–they either wanted to get to her father through her or they wanted to get her into bed. Sometimes both. The knowledge created a large knot in her chest.

"No. I can't have dinner with you tomorrow," she said. "Thank you, but I really need to mingle now."

Percy still held her hand in his. "Wait. I take back what I said. There's every need to thank me for saving you from Angus the lecher. If you agree to have dinner with me we'll call it even."

She wanted to smile at the "Angus the lecher" remark but schooled her face and raised an eyebrow at the impertinent Perseus. "I can't. I don't know you."

"We can remedy that." Perseus set her glass of wine on a passing tray and tugged gently on her hand. "Come with me."

Andi immediately resisted. "Where?"

Amusement curled one corner of Percy's mouth. A

dimple appeared in his left cheek. The urge to plant a kiss on that dimple made her blush. Percy's smile widened as if he had read her mind and she tried to pull her hand free but he kept hold. His large hand felt warm and strong and she had to admit that she liked the feel of it wrapped around her own.

"We won't leave the party, I promise. I want you to meet someone."

Andi's curiosity got the better of her. The last ten minutes had been the most interesting minutes of her adult life. "Okay. But no tricks. I can scream.'"

Percy's smile flashed wide and bright and her knees wobbled slightly. He chuckled softly, as if he knew full well the effect his smile had on her body. She stiffened in response.

"Come on." He led her through the throng to a handsome couple standing near the street edge of the roof terrace where a neatly trimmed box-shaped hedge protected people from falling off. Lights strung through the trees in Riverside Park reflected in the water below them.

Andi loved the long, narrow park strung out along the river and often walked it when she felt restless and needed to get out of her condo.

The male of the couple had a slight resemblance to Perseus although he stood a couple inches shorter and his eyes were an intelligent smoky gray instead of green. They looked similar enough to make her think they were related. There was no mistaking the aura of confidence they both oozed. An air of confidence that she deeply envied.

The wife wore her thick dark hair loose. The loose curls hung below her shapely, exposed shoulders, framing a strong yet attractive face. Her blue eyes were curious and friendly.

"Andromeda, I'd like you to meet my brother Zee and his

wife Pandora. They live in a beautiful stone house on Winter Street. Zee, Pan, this is Andromeda White. I just rescued her from an arrogant ass who wanted to take her on a dinner date that I'm sure included extra activities and now I'm trying to convince her to have dinner with me instead. I need you two to vouch for me."

Andi wanted to melt into the floor with embarrassment. She glanced around to see if anyone had overheard Perseus. The last thing she needed was for Angus to learn that there had been no previously arranged dinner date.

She risked a look at Zee and Pandora and saw that they were both smiling at her. Real smiles. Warm smiles. Compassionate smiles. She wasn't used to people smiling at her like that. She found herself smiling back.

"Call me Andi. Please. Andromeda is such a mouth full."

"It must be a trial sometimes," Pandora told her, "being so beautiful. I imagine you get hit on a lot by men you want nothing to do with. I'd be tempted to carry mace and just blast them in the face."

The unexpected comment made Andi laugh. No one had ever understood before how her beauty could be a burden. She decided she liked Pandora.

"It's worse when my father encourages them," she admitted. "He and Mother consider it their duty to find me a suitable mate, preferably one who'll contribute to the family business. And of course they want him to be rich so they usually set me up with either their business partners or successful athletes." Embarrassment struck again.

"I probably shouldn't have said that," she murmured. "It makes me sound pathetic."

"You aren't pathetic," Pandora assured her. "I support your right to acknowledge the truth. My own mother didn't live long enough to see me dating or married, and she never got to meet Zee. I never knew my father so I can't truly relate, but I can definitely sympathize."

She gave Andi another warm smile. "Why don't you and Percy both join us for dinner tomorrow night?"

"What?" Pandora asked, when Percy sent her a disgusted look. "Safety in numbers, Perce. The woman doesn't know you at all. This will give her a chance to find out if she wants to risk a real date with you."

"I'm a good guy." Perseus glared at his sister in law.

Pandora patted his arm. "Yes, you are. *We* know that, but we're family. Give Andi a chance to figure it out for herself."

Percy gave Zee an exasperated look. "Can't you control your wife?"

"Nope." Zee grinned at his brother. "I know better than to try. Nor would I even if I could. Besides, Pan has a point."

He turned to Andi. "We would be delighted and honored to have you grace our dinner table tomorrow night, but I should warn you that we have seven hooligan children so it will be a casual and noisy meal."

Seven children? Pandora didn't look old enough to have produced that many offspring. Andi smiled at Zee.

"That sounds wonderful. I love children and I'd love to have dinner with your family. Thank you for the invite." It was true. A meal that included children sounded great.

She turned to Perseus and held out her hand. "Thank you for . . . rescuing me, Mr. Perseus. I'll see you tomorrow night at—" She looked at Pandora.

"Five. We eat early because of the kids."

Andi nodded. "I'll be there at five."

Perseus took her hand. "Call me Percy, please. And I can pick you up. You don't know where they live."

Andi smiled. "My parents live in the yellow brick house next door to the stone house. Even if they didn't, everyone in

La Crosse knows the awesome house on Winter Street. It's magnificent."

Surprise crossed Pandora's face. "Your parents live next door? Did you grow up there? Why didn't we ever meet?"

Andi blushed. "Maybe because my folks sent me away to boarding schools and immediately after that I went to college." She shrugged. "I never met any of our neighbors growing up. I might be considered a La Crosse native but I know very few people. I'll see you tomorrow."

"I look forward to it. Dress casual." Pandora grinned at her. "There's no telling what kind of messes the kids will get into. They're what you call 'active'."

Andi pulled her hand free from Percy's and turned and walked away, feeling lighter and happier than she had in a long while. She was going to have dinner tomorrow night with a normal family, something she'd never done. Zee had said it would be casual and noisy.

It sounded wonderful.

Meals with her own family were either formal affairs with business-related guests or formal affairs with her parents. As an only child she'd been expected to dress for dinner and behave like an adult at the table which also meant not talking unless she was asked a direct question. Any questions she was asked were related to her performance in school. Dinners in the White home tended to be stiff and quiet affairs.

"Wow, that's some dress," Zee remarked as Andi walked away from them.

"*And* she looks incredible in it," his wife added. They both turned to Percy who was still watching Andi walk away through the crowd.

She did look incredible, he thought, but it wasn't just the dress. There was something about *her*. Andromeda White had a certain something that attracted him like metal filings to a magnet.

"Percy."

"What?" Percy dragged his eyes away from Andi's retreating back and looked at his sister in law.

Pandora's eyes had a knowing gleam in them. "I think Andi's co-workers have it wrong. She's not an ice queen, she's just protecting herself."

"Her father *wanted* her to go out with that arrogant old lecher." Percy shook his head in disgust. "I couldn't believe it. Why would he do that? She was giving the guy the cold shoulder until Daddy showed up and gave her some sort of signal."

"Daughters used to be married off in order to create strategic alliances and seal deals," Zee reminded him. "They were possessions used for bargaining."

"It's archaic," Percy grumbled.

"I think she could use a friend," Pandora said quietly. "You did a good thing tonight, Perce."

"It was entirely selfish. I couldn't bear the way that old lecher was pawing at her, like she was dessert and he had every right to her."

He located Andromeda in the crowd again. He felt somewhat stunned by his reaction to the woman. He wanted to protect her. He was also intrigued by her. And yes, he was fiercely attracted to her.

When he turned back to his brother and sister in law they were both grinning at him.

# CHAPTER 5

ANDI'S FEET were killing her. Her facial muscles hurt from holding a smile all night. Her shoulders and neck felt stiff. She could have wept with relief when eleven o'clock rolled around and Charles showed up with the car.

She rode down in the elevator with her mother and one other couple while her father said a few last good-byes. Given the speculative look in her mother's eyes she felt grateful for their presence. Unfortunately the reprieve only lasted until they were all seated in the Mercedes and Charles was headed toward her condo.

"So Andromeda, your father tells me you made a dinner date for tomorrow night."

Andi removed the earrings and handed them to her mother to put away. She didn't want to talk about Perseus with her parents. She wanted to keep him and Zee and Pandora all to herself, at least for a little while.

"You should have let us know, dear. Your father could have headed off Angus's dinner invite and avoided a scene. Turn around so I can get the necklace."

Andromeda complied. She shivered as the long chain of diamonds was removed from her back.

"Tell us about this man you are having dinner with."

Unfortunately Andi knew from bitter experience that her mother would persist with the questions until she had milked every scrap of information there was to be had. Nothing was sacred or off limits.

Cass's ability to worm secrets and knowledge from anyone had made her a valuable asset to her father's business. Andi also knew that her father had already told her mother all about the scene with Angus Ames.

"He's just someone I met tonight," she answered, trying for nonchalance and bending to remove her heels so her mother couldn't see her face.

"Your father told me he introduced himself as the brother of a potential new business partner."

"I guess." She shrugged one shoulder and looked out the window, hoping her mother would take the hint. Fat chance of that. Her mother was like a terrier with a rat when she got a whiff of something she didn't know.

"I don't know anything about his brother," Andi added.

"How did you meet him?"

"He introduced himself to me." Shoes off, Andi sat back up and wiggled her sore toes. She pretended not to notice her mother studying her face with narrowed eyes.

"Angus Ames is important to Cepheus White Sports," Cass said mildly. "It's not a good idea to anger him."

"I know that, Mother. I didn't do it on purpose."

What about me? she wondered silently. Wasn't she important? Didn't it matter that Angus Ames creeped her out and she didn't *want* to have dinner with him?

"Getting exclusive rights to the Olympian franchise is also important," her mother continued. She reached out and lightly patted Andi's knee. "Good work. We'll expect you to learn everything you can from . . . Perseus, was it? . . . yes?"

At Andi's nod she went on. "Ask Perseus about Zee's business during your dinner date. It wouldn't hurt to learn about the brother's personal life as well."

"And then spill all to you." Andi couldn't keep the bitterness from her voice.

"Naturally. The more information we have on Zee the better deal we'll be able to negotiate with him. Where is Perseus taking you to eat? Someplace nice, I hope. Preferably someplace where you'll be seen. It never hurts to be seen with a good looking man. I'll call Cat at the paper and have her stop by the restaurant and snap a shot of you both dining. Wear something photo worthy."

Andi suppressed a shudder. Cat, her mother's contact at the paper, was only too happy to curry favor with the White's. In exchange for featured write ups and their pictures in the society and business sections Cat got invited to all of her parents' events and parties. Andi had tried to avoid Cat's camera that evening but she didn't know if she'd succeeded. The woman could be sneaky.

"Andromeda. Your mother asked you where Perseus is taking you to dinner tomorrow."

"I don't know. He didn't say." Not a lie since Zee and Pandora were the ones who had invited her to their house. "Perseus doesn't live in La Crosse so he probably needs to ask his brother for restaurant recommendations." There. That sounded reasonable.

Cass drummed her long, elegant fingers on the leather seat. She didn't frown. Her mother never frowned because she was worried about creating lines on her still beautiful face.

"Not knowing where you're going is a problem." She

thought for a minute, then leaned toward Andi. "I know what we'll do. Call me as soon as you get to the restaurant and I'll have Cat standing by. As soon as I know the location I'll call her." She leaned back in the seat with a satisfied nod. "That will work."

"What if he takes me someplace out of town? Forget Cat please, Mother. Let me have a date without being stalked by your pet photographer."

"Andromeda! Don't speak to your mother that way. I insist that you apologize."

The car drew up in front of Andi's condo. She gathered up her shoes and the clutch and reached for the door handle. "I'm sorry if I offended you Mother, but to be honest I don't like having my picture plastered all over the paper. I'm not a publicity hound like you and Dad are. Good night."

She opened the door as Charles reached for it. He took her elbow instead and helped her out of the vehicle. Her parents were sputtering behind her.

"Bully for you, Miss Andi," Charles whispered into her ear as he steered her toward the condo entrance. "It's about time you stood up for yourself." He squeezed her elbow gently and let her go.

"Good night, Miss Andi," he said loudly. "You take care of yourself now."

Andi leaned down and planted a kiss on the driver's smooth cheek. "Thank you, Charles. Good night." She walked barefoot into her building, not caring who saw her carrying her shoes.

Once inside the privacy of her condo Andi fell into a slump on her couch. She didn't know whether to laugh or cry. She assumed her parents loved her but she wasn't totally convinced of that.

Cepheus and Cass White were all about their business

and they used everything at their disposal to grow that business, including their only child.

Andi knew that her parents considered her beauty–which was an accident of fate and not a personal accomplishment–an important asset. They had no qualms about exploiting it. They often roped her into dinners with clients and business partners despite her discomfort in social situations.

Her mother kept telling her that she simply needed more practice but she'd been practicing since she turned sixteen and she still hadn't developed the social élan that her mother possessed in spades.

The hell of it was, she let her parents get away with using her. Was she so afraid of losing their love that she compromised herself to gain their approval?

Andi blew out a heavy sigh. Yep. Pathetic as it may be, her parents were all she had.

She hugged one of the intricately quilted couch pillows to her chest and looked out at the river spooling to the south. A barge was passing beneath the Winter Street bridge, the original bridge that crossed the river proper and after two miles of wetlands and islands, linked Wisconsin to Minnesota.

The double arcs of the bridge and the massive barge were both lit up. The tug wielded a spotlight and red and green running lights.

Andi never tired of watching the constant traffic on the river and often whiled away a lonely evening doing just that, but tonight it did nothing to soothe her thoughts.

Why had she agreed to have dinner with Zee and Pandora? She wanted to call and cancel but she'd forgotten to get a phone number from any of them. Stupid.

She never did learn what Percy did for work. She'd been so sure he played some sport when she saw him outside the elevator. Even in his suit she could see the athletic build-broad shoulders and long, strong legs. He moved with the easy grace of an athlete as well.

She had felt the strength in his hands yet he'd been very gentle when he touched her. Her face flushed at the memory of his large warm hand clasped around hers.

She couldn't have dinner with them. She'd make a fool of herself. She always did. She became tongue-tied around people and couldn't talk. It wasn't a problem with the men her parents fixed her up with. Those guys were only too happy to talk about themselves.

"Crap." Andi tossed down the pillow and stood. She needed to get out of the dress and into her pajamas. She had a good book, a new romance by Jill Shalvis. She read a lot of romances. They gave her hope that there was more to life, just not her life.

She heard a tiny cry as she walked by the bathroom.

"Oh! I'm so sorry, little one. I forgot all about you." Andi scooped the angry kitten out of the tub and cuddled her high on her chest. The kitten tucked her head into Andi's neck and began kneading against her.

"I've got you. Don't you worry." It felt good having another warm body in the condo besides her own, she thought as she hurriedly dressed. Maybe she should keep the kitten. Then she'd have someone waiting for her to come home after work.

She lifted the kitten so they were eye to eye. "What do you think? Do you want to stay with me or go to the animal shelter and hope someone adopts you?"

Golden eyes blinked at her and the kitten mewed.

"Good choice. Let's go to Wally World and get you some food and stuff. Get you officially moved in." She found an empty basket, placed a dish towel in the bottom and placed the kitten on the towel.

"There. You can ride in that." Excitement coursed through Andi's veins. She'd never had a pet before.

"You're going to need a name and it needs to be one that fits." She gave the kitten a critical look. "You look like Halloween with all that black and orange fur and those big gold eyes. And you scared me in the alley where I found you. I think I'll call you Spook. Do you like that name?"

The kitten spied its tail and spun a circle in the basket trying to catch it, making Andi laugh. When had she last found something to laugh out loud about? Smiling, she headed to the store with her new roommate.

# CHAPTER 6

IT WAS four-thirty on Saturday night and Andi still didn't know what to wear to her dinner date. Pandora and Zee had said "casual" but casual encompassed a wide variety of styles. A sundress and low heels? She tried on four and discarded them all.

Jean mini skirt with tee shirt? Cotton twill mini skirt with short sleeved button-front blouse? Long skirt? Shorts? Argh!

No shorts. They felt too revealing. So did the mini skirts. The long, gypsy-style skirt with peasant blouse made her feel like she was trying too hard. Jeans felt *too* casual. She gave a small scream of self-disgust and scooped Spook off the pile of clothing she had tossed on her bed.

"I need to find something in the next ten minutes, Spook. Help me out here."

The kitten licked her chin with his rough tongue. Andi had finally remembered to look at Spook's privates to see if she'd rescued a male or female kitten. Turned out Spook was a he. Fortunately Spook was an asexual name and worked for either gender.

"You're no help." Andi set the kitten in the middle of the pile of discarded clothes. He pounced and attacked the large buttons on one of the skirts, making her laugh.

Time was running out.

"Screw it." She grabbed a pair of olive capris and a white tee and slipped them on, added a beaded belt and a silver and turquoise bracelet and decided against earrings. She left her hair down but tucked a barrette into her tote in case she wanted to fasten it back later. A pair of white sneakers and she was ready to go.

Except that she wasn't. Her stomach was tied up in knots from nerves and she was already hyperventilating at the thought of eating a meal with strangers.

They'd expect her to talk to them.

"I am so not cut out for this kind of thing," she muttered. If she had only thought to get a phone number she could have cancelled.

"Coward." She looked at Spook. He had finished playing and was nesting in the skirt, curled up into a tiny black and orange ball. "What am I going to do with you?"

She was trying out the new kitty litter box in the bathroom, looking for the ideal spot to place Spook's toilet. She should shut him up in the bath with his food and water dishes while she was gone but she didn't want to. He'd voiced his displeasure over that very thing the night before.

She frowned at the kitten, frowned at the clock, then made up her mind. "You're coming with me." She wouldn't feel so outnumbered with Spook at her side. Besides, Pandora and Zee said they had seven young children. Kids liked kittens.

At five on the dot Andi turned into the stone castle's driveway. She had waited on a side street until one minute to five because she didn't want to be early, fully aware that she was behaving like a nutcase.

Grabbing the gift-bagged bottle of wine, her tote, and Spook's travel crate she walked up the flagstone walk to the front door and gathered her courage–again.

It felt strange ringing the bell of a place she'd admired and made up stories about when she was a young girl. She could hear the chimes echoing somewhere deep inside the house. She noted with approval the tall, thick hedge separating the yard from her parents. At least her folks wouldn't be able to see her car. She wouldn't put it past her mother to invite herself over if she knew Andi was dining there.

The thought made Andi's nerves spike again. She turned back to the door. Where was everyone? Had she gotten the time or the day wrong? What if they weren't expecting her and she was intruding?

The door opened as she turned away.

"You must be Andromeda. Come on in." The woman smiled and stepped back to let Andi enter a large entry hall. She was short and pleasantly round with soft brown hair and even features. Andi guessed her to be in her mid-thirties. The woman held out her hand to shake, then noticed that Andi's were full and laughed.

"I'm Samantha but please call me Sam. Everyone else does. I look after the house for Pandora and Zee. They're all out back. They got playing a game of whiffle ball with the kids and won't quit until there's a clear winner. Follow me." She took off down the wide, black marble-tiled hallway toward the rear of the house.

Andi hesitated a moment, then started after her. She hadn't expected servants. Servants meant formal–she knew that from her mother's house. Casual in a formal house was different from casual in a normal household. She should have gone with the long skirt and peasant blouse. A weight pressed on her chest and she had trouble catching her breath.

She passed a formal dining room on her left with a crystal chandelier hanging from a punched tin ceiling. A trompe l'oeil painting of an Italian villa set in a vineyard covered the far wall and a massive polished cherry table filled the space. No places had been set on the table yet.

"Can I help set the table?" she asked. Maybe if she felt useful she wouldn't be quite so nervous. Plus there was the added bonus that it would delay joining everyone.

"What?" Sam laughed and shook her head. "We only use that room when the relatives visit. We'll be eating in the kitchen tonight. Family style. I hope that doesn't bother you." She stopped smiling and gave Andi a speculative look.

Andi's shoulders relaxed slightly. "No. I'd prefer the kitchen, actually. Um, I brought this wine for Pandora and Zee." She thrust the decorative bottle bag towards Sam.

"What a lovely gesture." Sam took the bottle and led Andi into the coziest kitchen she'd ever seen. "They'll appreciate it, I can assure you. Zee and Pan both enjoy their wine."

Andi wasn't listening. "Wow. I *love* this room." The kitchen ran the entire width of the back of the house. An old red AGA stove sat against the wall to her right with a pale limestone fireplace anchoring the wall at the opposite end of the room. An overstuffed couch covered in a faded floral pattern and three beat-up, brown leather chairs faced the fireplace. There was no fire at the moment but Andi could easily imagine how cozy it would be with one snapping and popping on a chilly evening.

The kitchen smelled delicious, reminding Andi of one of her favorite meals from boarding school. "Is that macaroni and cheese I smell?" Her eyes widened when she spied the cake platter sitting on the granite counter. "And chocolate cake?"

"Yep. Not exactly guest fare but it's Danny's turn to pick the meal and he always picks his favorite. I hope you don't mind."

"Are you kidding? I *love* mac and cheese. And chocolate cake is my favorite." She grinned at Sam, a genuine smile. "That's my all-time fav meal."

Sam smiled back at her. "That's a relief. Percy was a little worried about how you'd take it but traditions are hard to break around here. Saturdays are kid's choice night. There would have been a major battle if Percy had asked Danny to give up his night."

"I'm glad he didn't. I would have been very disappointed to miss it." Andi wandered the kitchen toward the fireplace. Sturdy, plain white pottery, its surface crackled and discolored with age, filled a massive walnut buffet that rose to the ceiling and filled a large portion of the inside wall. By the looks of it she'd guess it had been there nearly as long as the house.

A long farm table sat in the center of the room with benches on each of the long sides and captain's chairs at each end, its scarred oak surface already set for twelve.

Twelve?

"Seven kids. Five adults. Danny had to count it all out three times before he was confident he set the table right."

Andi hadn't realized she'd spoken out loud. "I can't believe Pandora has seven children."

"She doesn't. Four of them belong to me."

Movement drew Andi's eyes to the back wall of windows. A whiffle ball game was indeed in progress. The children ranged in age from a very young girl toddling across the makeshift diamond to a brown haired teenage boy playing catcher.

Perseus stood on the pitcher's mound dressed in grass stained cargo shorts and a snug tee with sock-less sneakers on his feet. His brown hair was mussed and he appeared to be enjoying himself.

He was doing an elaborate, mock wind-up with a hole-filled, plastic whiffle ball. She could hear the others either jeering or hooting as he tried to stare down Pandora who stood tapping the plate with a fat red bat, grinning at him.

Andi felt much better about her capris and tee shirt when she saw that Pandora wore a pair of ragged cutoff jeans and a simple tank top. Her thick black hair was pulled back in a messy ponytail

Perseus let the ball fly. Pandora took a big swing and connected. The ball flew into the air and Pandora streaked for a bright orange frisbee marking first base. Zee took off from second base, scooping up the toddler who had plunked herself on the baseline between second and third. Everyone was yelling.

Zee made it to third with the toddler. Pandora stood safe on first and hooted at Perseus. She looked toward the house and saw Andi standing in the windows and pointed. Andi hadn't even realized that she had moved closer to the windows to watch the game.

Perseus turned and beckoned her outside.

Andi shook her head no and stepped back from the window. Perseus tossed the ball to the ground and trotted toward the house, his legs eating up the ground. A moment later he burst through a door near the Aga.

"Come on, Andi," he said. "I need you out there. Zee and Pandora always team up and leave me with all the young-sters." His grin belied the begging tone of his words and made her think of mischievous little boys and puppy dogs. Warm and friendly and totally irresistible.

"I can't, Perseus." She shook her head. "Really. Thank you for asking but I'll just watch."

Despite her automatic refusal she wanted to play. She'd always enjoyed sports at school. She liked to be active and she liked games. She'd even been fairly decent at them. But it had been several years since she'd played at anything and she didn't want to embarrass herself in front of people she didn't even know.

More accurately, she didn't want to embarrass herself in front of Percy, she amended. She smiled and hoped that would be the end of it but Percy advanced on her with a gleam in his eye.

"Not taking no for an answer."

# CHAPTER 7

Perseus had no intention of letting Andi slide out of playing. Her toned body told him she was no stranger to sports.

Before Andi realized what he intended he slid her tote off her shoulder and took Spook's carrier from her hand.

"Take care of these, will you please, Sam?" He handed off the items to Samantha and grabbed Andi's hand, pulling her toward the door. Not wanting to make a scene, she allowed him to pull her along.

They passed through a large, tiled mudroom filled with jackets and footwear, balls and kites and toys, and exited out the back door into a pleasant, shaded yard. A beautiful stone carriage house filled one back corner of the yard. Tall hedges of lilacs and something Andi couldn't identify fenced the yard and provided privacy from the neighbors.

"Andi's playing for my team," Perseus boomed.

"No, really, I–"

Perseus leaned in close, his warm green eyes filled with laughter. "Don't tell me you're afraid to play a little whiffle ball with a bunch of young kids," he challenged. "Take second base. Don't step on any children." He gently squeezed her hand then dropped it and walked back to the pitcher's mound.

Andi's pride forced her across the yard to a day-glo green frisbee that marked second base. Zee and Pandora waved hello to her from first and third. The boy playing first asked Perseus if Andi was any good.

"Don't know," came the reply. "But she's ours."

For some reason the words warmed Andi's heart. She jutted out her chin and bent her knees slightly, ready to field the ball. She could do this. Percy was right–these were only kids. And Zee and Pandora. And Percy. *Focus on the kids, Andi, or you'll tense up.*

A teen boy who looked suspiciously like a slightly older version of the first baseman and the catcher stepped up to the plate and took a few hard swings with the bat. Zee encouraged him to "hit me home, Luke."

Perseus pitched the ball and Luke hit it between second and third base. A young girl with curly black hair picked up the ball and threw it four feet toward Andi. The girl beamed as Perseus complimented her. Andi ran for the ball and dove back to second base a moment before Pandora slid in.

"Safe!" shouted Zee from home plate.

"Out!" shouted Perseus stepping off the pitching mound. "Andi beat her to the base. That's three outs. We're up."

Pandora grinned at Andi as they got to their feet. "Next time I'll be a little faster."

Andi grinned back. "Maybe."

The rest of the game passed in a blur of shouts and laughter. Andi was flushed and grass-stained by the time Sam came to call them all to dinner. There was a great deal of gentle ribbing as everyone trooped inside and washed up for a late dinner.

"I know we promised you food at five," Pandora said with

an apologetic look, "but we tend to be a competitive family. We have a hard time quitting in the middle of any game."

"You were great, Andi." Zack the catcher, younger brother to Luke, smiled at her and she smiled back. She'd had fun and her self conscious nerves had disappeared.

"Thank you, Zack. I thought you played great too." The boy blushed at the compliment.

"I think you've made yourself a friend for life," Perseus whispered into her ear.

Andi pushed down a tiny thrill from the feel of his soft breath on her ear and took a seat on one of the table benches.

She found herself sitting between Perseus and the young girl who had thrown the ball to her. Mia turned out to be Pandora and Zee's precocious four year old daughter. The two year old toddler was her younger sister Ariel and she had a six year old brother named Greg and a cat named Squirt. Mia had gleefully filled Andi in on all this while waiting for her food.

Dinner was as noisy an affair as the whiffle ball game had been, with a great deal of chatter and laughter and food passed around. People talked across and down the table with no regard for talking over anyone else. Drinks in sippy cups and wine glasses were passed, plates filled and emptied.

Andi soaked up the comfortable atmosphere. Her mother would be appalled, she thought with an inward grin. Not only that the young children were allowed to eat with the adults, but that they were encouraged to freely speak at the dinner table.

Meals at her parents' house had always been stiff, quiet affairs when she was home for the holidays.

"Quarter for your thoughts."

Andi looked over to see Percy's green eyes studying her. She was painfully aware of his powerful thigh pressing against hers. She wanted to move it away but had no place to move to with Mia pressed up against her opposite side.

"A quarter?" her voice sounded a little breathless. She took a sip of wine and tried again. "I thought the going price for thoughts was a penny."

Perseus shrugged a grass-stained shoulder. "Inflation. Plus I figured I had a better chance of you honestly telling me what you were thinking just then if I made it worth your while."

Andi smiled. Percy was a genuinely nice man. She decided to tell him the truth. "I was thinking about how different this is from the meals I had with my parents as a kid. I was only allowed to speak at the table if I was spoken to first and no one ever laughed. Conversation was always about my grades or classes or Dad's business or lectures from my mother."

She realized suddenly that everyone had gone quiet. Eleven faces were turned toward her. They had all heard her.

"Why didn't they let you talk?" Zack asked. "Were you being punished?"

Andi sputtered a laugh and wished she had kept her thoughts to herself. "No, I was a very well behaved little girl, Zack. My parents believe that children are meant to be seen and not heard. Plus I didn't have any sisters or brothers to talk to. You are all very fortunate."

"Sounds awful." Luke gave an affectionate poke to his sister Sarah who was sitting beside him. "This chatterbox would never have survived in your house. She can't keep quiet for more than ten seconds."

"Can too."

"Can't."

"Can too."

"Show me."

After that everyone went back to talking. Andi took a deep breath and took another sip of wine. She never should have let her guard down, she chided herself. She had brought a note of seriousness to a happy family dinner.

A large warm hand grasped the hand that sat in her lap.

"That must have been very difficult for you," Percy said quietly. "Children are meant to be loud and boisterous and full of life. Is that why you act so reserved?"

"I–" Andi felt tears pressing into her eyes and willed them away. "I think I need to head home," she said, pulling her hand free. She climbed off the bench and stepped back from the table.

"Thank you, everyone. It was a pleasure meeting you all. Dinner was delicious. And thank you for including me in your whiffle ball game. I had fun."

"Next time maybe your team will win," Zee told her with a grin. Everyone hooted.

The pressure in Andi's eyes eased and she smiled back. "Next time my team *will* win." Everyone hooted again, making her feel much better. She preferred to leave on a positive note than a sad one.

She scooped up Spook who had been doing his best to get at Pandora's cat Squirt. The older cat had wisely retreated to the couch back, well out of the kitten's reach. She placed Spook in his carrier, grabbed her tote and headed for the hall.

"Don't get up," she told Sam when the other woman started to leave the table. "I can let myself out."

"I'll walk her to her car." Percy rose. "Make sure you save another piece of cake for me," he told Sam. He took the carrier from Andi's hand so she had no choice but to follow him down the hall.

Neither Percy nor Andi spoke until she stood beside her

car. She reached for Spook's carrier. "I can take that," she told him. She desperately wanted to get out of there before she embarrassed herself again.

Percy released his hold on the cage. "I didn't mean to run you off by asking a personal question."

Andi shook her head while she avoided looking at him. "You didn't. I really do need to get home. Spook needs his dinner and I've stayed longer than I intended." She risked a look up and could see by the compassionate look in Percy's eyes that he knew she was lying. To her relief he let it pass.

Percy placed a hand on the top edge of her car door, a move that prevented her from opening it. She felt the pulse in her neck kick up a beat.

"I'd like to see you again, Andi. Would you have dinner with me one night this week?"

He wanted to see her again? Why?

"Because you're an attractive, intelligent, interesting woman and I like you. Why wouldn't I want to see you?"

She'd spoken her thoughts out loud again. She really needed to watch that.

She turned her head and found Percy's face less than a foot from her own. He stood so close that she could see golden highlights in his deep green eyes.

Those eyes were smiling at her. Heck, his whole face was smiling at her. She couldn't help smiling back.

"I have to work."

"You also have to eat dinner. I'll pick you up Monday night around seven and I'll get you home early since it's a work night. Say, 'Yes, Percy.'" His gaze dropped to her mouth.

"Yes, Percy." Was he thinking about kissing her? The possibility made her feel a little breathless. "I'd like that. Do you know where I live?"

"Don't tell me. I'll impress you with my detective skills." He pulled back and removed his hand from her car.

No kiss then. She tried to ignore her disappointment. "Okay. Seven on Monday. I'll be ready." She loaded everything into her car and backed out of the driveway.

She had a date. A real date with someone who wasn't a client of her father's. A date with a man who thought she was intelligent and interesting. She felt giddy with happiness and wished the date was for the next evening. She couldn't remember the last time she had looked forward to something with excited anticipation.

She drove back to her condo with a smile plastered on her face.

CHAPTER 8

ANDI'S MOTHER called at nine on the dot Sunday morning, the earliest her mother considered "decent" for a weekend phone call.

"How was dinner, dear? You must tell me all about it."

Andi twitched the yarn she had tied to the handle of a wooden spoon in front of Spook's face. She was stretched out on her couch, basking in the morning sunshine and reliving the previous evening. The kitten lunged at the string and flipped on his back, biting at the fierce string. Andi bit back a laugh and answered her mother.

"I enjoyed myself. We had macaroni and cheese and chocolate cake."

"What? What kind of man feeds a woman macaroni and cheese on a first date? Or any date for that matter. I hope you grilled him and at least made it worth your while."

The sunshine seemed to dim a little. "I enjoyed myself, Mother," Andi repeated. "And no, I didn't grill Perseus." She heard a heavy sigh over the phone and knew she'd disappointed her mother once again.

"Never mind. You'll come to the house for dinner tonight. Stella will make up for last night's dinner."

Stella was her parents' cook and Charles's sister. Andi knew her almost as well as Charles. She liked Stella. The woman was a fabulous cook and made dinner with her parents a treat. Of course her mother wouldn't accept anyone less than a top chef. Cass had a need to be the best at and have the best of everything.

"I don't need Stella to make up for my dinner, Mother. I told you, I *enjoyed* myself. I'd rather not go out tonight. I've been out the last two nights and I need to catch up on a few things before the work week."

She didn't actually have anything that needed her attention but her mother didn't need to know that. Laundry was caught up and the condo was clean. Andi was enjoying a rare day of relaxation. Mostly she wanted to lie around and think about Perseus and play with Spook. Maybe take a walk along the river.

"Whatever you have to do can wait. I insist that you join us for dinner. Dress appropriately. We'll expect you at six forty-five."

Her mother hung up before Andi could argue any further. Frustrated, she tossed her phone to the other end of the couch and scooped up the kitten. Spook was still a little wild from attacking the yarn and he sunk his baby claws into her hand.

"Ouch! Those claws hurt, mister." She stroked his back until he calmed down and lay purring on her chest.

"I am such a pushover," she told Spook. Had she ever said no to her mother? If she had Andi was ninety nine point nine percent sure that her mother had ignored her. She groaned. Dinner with her parents was the last thing she wanted to do that evening.

She spent the rest of the day relaxing and rang her parents' bell at exactly six forty-five. No one simply walked into Cass White's house, even if they were her only child.

Charles opened the door and eyed her. "Your mother said you'd be here and on time."

Andi stepped into the wide foyer and bussed him lightly on the cheek. "Hello to you too, Charles. Are my parents in the living room?"

"They are." He closed the door. "Along with their guest."

Andi had started for the living room but she stopped and walked back to where Charles stood. "Guest?"

"You know your mother. Ever optimistic."

Andi's shoulders slumped. Her mother had been setting her up with blind dates in what felt like forever despite Andi's protests. She looked longingly at the front door. "I don't suppose I can sneak back out."

"Nope. They know you're here. Remember, just because your mother thinks a man is suitable that doesn't mean you have to date him." Charles preceded her into Cass's formal living room.

"Andromeda is here," he announced. He turned and left the room, giving her a smile and a broad wink as he left.

Easy for him to find humor in the situation, Andi grumped to herself. Charles wasn't the one who had to make small talk with the men her mother set her up with. She took a deep breath and pasted a smile on her face. She had tomorrow night to look forward to. She could get through this. She knew the drill–smile and act interested then politely decline any attempt to see her again.

The living room ran almost the full depth of the house. The oak floors were polished to a high sheen. Three blue oriental rugs delineated separate seating areas, each one anchored by modern, pale linen-covered sectional sofas and matching arm chairs. A mix of modern and traditional art hung on the pale gold walls. It was a room Andi had always found a little too stiff for comfort.

When she realized who her parents' guest was she almost turned and left. Only the impeccable manners that had been drilled into her for as long as she could remember kept her there.

"Andi, you remember Angus Ames." Her mother's voice clearly said that she'd *better* remember Mr. Ames.

Andi stepped forward and stretched out her hand. "Don't be silly, Mother. Of course I remember Angus. We spoke on Friday night."

Angus clasped her hand between both of his. His fingers were slim and smooth, his nails perfectly manicured and buffed to a shine, his touch cool. Andi couldn't resist comparing them to Percy's roughened, warm hands.

"It's a pleasure to see you again, Andi." Angus smiled, revealing perfect teeth that looked a little too white against his salon tan. "I trust your date last night treated you well? What was his name? Something ridiculous I seem to remember."

Andi picked up on the contempt beneath Angus's haughty tone. She knew he had not been introduced to Percy although he would have heard Percy introduce himself to her father. She pulled her hand from his and walked over to the drink cart to pour herself a glass of wine. She was going to need a drink to get through dinner, she could already tell.

"As a matter of fact I had a very nice time," she said. She could feel three sets of eyes boring into her back. She sipped her wine and turned to face them. "I thought you were leaving town today, Angus."

"Your mother convinced me to stay another day and join

you all for dinner. I couldn't turn down such an attractive invitation, especially once she told me you'd be here."

*I just bet you couldn't.* She was going to have to have another talk with her mother about setting her up with men she didn't like. Apparently none of the other talks had taken.

Andi pasted on the social smile that didn't reach her eyes but Angus didn't notice. He was too busy running his eyes down her body. She had worn a simple light cotton wrap sundress in soft coral that hugged her curves. Her parents always dressed for dinner so she'd worn something dressy enough to satisfy her mother but also comfortable. She wished now she had chosen her oldest pair of jeans and a tee shirt.

Crossing the room to rejoin her parents, Andi deliberately chose a chair set slightly apart from Angus. "So, what are we talking about?" she asked brightly.

"We were just discussing a new line of sleepwear that Angus is going to produce for us," Cepheus said. "We've done well with the infant and toddler lines. I want to expand into adult wear–unisex boxers and tank tops."

The business talk carried them through drinks and into Cass's elegant dining room and dinner. Andi was beginning to think she might escape unscathed when Angus turned the conversation to more personal matters when dessert was served.

"I extended my stay another night, Andi. I'd like you to have dinner with me tomorrow night. I've made reservations at Morocco's."

Andi had eaten at Morocco's–rated La Crosse's best restaurant five years running–with her parents several times for business dinners. The food was excellent, with a James Beard award chef. Besides the main dining room it had romantic, private alcoves, ideal for couples.

She did not want to have dinner there with Angus. She smiled at him and swallowed the mouthful of smooth orange sherbet she knew Stella had made just for her. Baked goods weren't allowed in the White household because they were fattening so Stella had come up with an alternative for when the younger Andi came home for holidays.

"I'm sorry, Angus, but I already have plans for tomorrow night," she told him. She refrained from saying "perhaps another time" because she didn't want him to ask her again.

There was no mistaking the way the skin around Angus's eyes tightened. He was obviously not pleased with her answer.

"I'm beginning to think you're avoiding me, Andi," he said softly. He turned to Andi's mother. "What do you think, Cass? Is your daughter avoiding me?"

"Certainly not, Angus. Why would she?" Cass hadn't touched her sherbet. It lay in her shallow dessert bowl, a growing puddle of pale orange. Unlike Andi Cass never ate dessert. She was proud of her slim figure and sacrificed desserts as well as putting in long hours in her home gym to maintain it.

"I'm sure your plans can be changed to accommodate Angus, Andromeda. You'll simply have to make your excuses for tomorrow. Something more important has come up."

Andi heard the steel in her mother's voice. Coupled with the fact that her mother had just addressed her as Andromeda warned her that her mother was angry and digging in for a battle. One Andi had never before won.

She took another spoonful of the sherbet, taking time to enjoy the cold sweetness in her mouth. She wondered if Perseus liked sherbet. She thought he probably did. Any man who loved chocolate cake and macaroni and cheese would like orange sherbet as well.

"Do you like macaroni and cheese?" she asked Angus suddenly.

"What?" He looked surprised by the question. "Only the poor and uneducated eat macaroni and cheese." He narrowed his eyes at her. "Why? Where did that question come from?"

Andi carefully set down her spoon and shook her head. "It doesn't matter. I just wondered what you like to eat when you aren't trying to impress others."

"Andromeda!" Cass's face had gone white. Even her father looked shocked.

"I beg your pardon? Did you just insult me?" Angus looked as if he couldn't believe what he'd just heard. His face flushed a dull red beneath his tan and his hand gripped the stem of his wine glass so hard Andi wondered if it would snap.

She supposed a man like Angus Ames rarely had anyone disagree with him or say anything to him that wasn't pleasant social bullshit.

Without thinking about what she was doing she found herself standing. "I have to go now," she said. "I have a long day ahead of me tomorrow. Thank you for dinner, Mother. I'll let myself out."

She heard only silence behind her as she crossed the room. Unfortunately her mother regained her composure. "Excuse me a moment, Angus. I need a word with my daughter."

Andi forced her feet not to run. She had stood up to her mother for the first time in her life and she would see it through. She only wished her hands weren't trembling.

"Andromeda White, don't you run away from me."

Andi took a deep breath to steady her nerves and turned around. "What do you want, Mother? I won't have dinner with Angus Ames. He's at least twenty years older than I am and I don't like the man."

Her mother came to a stop in front of her, blue eyes blazing. "What does age or liking have to do with anything? Angus Ames is your father's biggest supplier. We need to keep him happy, and if that means you have to give up a few hours of your precious time to have dinner with him then *you will do it*." The last few words came out on an angry hiss.

"No." Andi looked at her mother and felt her nerves settle. "If you are so concerned about keeping Ames happy then why don't you have dinner with him? He's more your age anyway."

'Because he wants you, you ungrateful girl."

"That's exactly it, Mother. He doesn't just want me for a dinner companion. I'm not an object for sale or barter or whatever you call this. *I don't like Angus Ames.* Do not try to set me up with him again."

Andi turned and walked to the front door. Charles stood waiting to let her out, his face expressionless. She knew he couldn't avoid hearing every word.

"You heard?" she asked him quietly.

"Have a good evening, Miss Andi," he said with a stiff nod. He opened the door for her. As he was closing the door behind her he leaned out. "Bully for you, girl. It's about time you put a stop to your mother pimping you out."

Andi stood on the front step feeling as if she'd been poleaxed. She had never considered her mother's machinations as pimping before but the term fit like a snug leather glove.

She bit back a sudden laugh.

Wouldn't her oh-so-proper mother be shocked to hear herself referred to as a pimp!

Her mood felt much lighter on her way back to her condo and Spook.

Something momentous had happened to her at dinner, something that had changed her in ways she didn't understand yet but was anxious to explore.

And tomorrow she had another date with Perseus. For the first time since she'd started working for Cepheus White Sports she was actually looking forward to going to work.

"ONE SEVENTY-NINE, one eighty, one eighty-one, one eighty-TWO." Andi pulled open the fire escape door to the seventh floor and let herself into the customer service department. The lights were on and she could hear operators already taking orders in their blue-gray cubicles. She was usually one of the first to arrive but thanks to the scene at her parents' she'd had a difficult time sleeping the night before and had gotten a late start.

As she walked toward her office she caught the eye of one of the operators, a short, slightly pudgy woman with curly red hair.

The woman's eyes slid away. There was no change of expression on her face, no acknowledgement that she'd seen and recognized Andi.

Andi walked by the cubicle which had a "Hang in There" cat poster and two photos of the woman with a man on her desk. Husband? Boyfriend? She knew nothing about any of her co-workers who weren't really co-workers.

The friendships she'd hoped to forge by working on the seventh floor instead of the eighth had not come to pass and she had no one to blame but herself. She knew that. She just didn't know what to do about it.

She passed the next cubicle which was still empty and stopped. Here was the perfect opportunity to step outside her comfort zone.

She took a deep breath to steady herself and walked back to the woman who looked up at her in surprise.

"Miss White? Do you need something?"

Andi stuck out her right hand. "Call me Andi. Please. I thought it was about time I started meeting some of the people I work with. I know it's taken me a while but I wasn't sure how to go about it you see."

"Oh." The woman stood. "I'm Maggie Hoffmann. It's nice to finally meet you."

Andi grimaced at Maggie's slight emphasis on *finally*. "I can imagine what everyone thinks, me being the owner's daughter and all but I never wanted to work here and then Cepheus insisted I have an office instead of a cubicle and . . . shit. Too much information. Sorry." She realized she was rambling and clamped her mouth shut.

Maggie studied her. "It can't be easy being the boss's daughter," she said after a long moment. "I'll admit I've been curious about you but I didn't dare approach you. You seemed so aloof and wrapped up in your work."

"I can see how you'd think that, because I am. Aloof and wrapped up in my work that is. I mean, I'm not really aloof. It's just that everyone here seems to be friends and I didn't know how to break into that. I'm not only the boss's daughter, I'm an outsider."

Andi paused. "To be honest I'm not really wrapped up in my work either." She grimaced. "I mean, I am, because I always try to do my best, but I'm not, because this isn't what I want to be doing with my life." She huffed out a breath. "I'm not making any sense, am I?"

"Actually, it's good to find out that you're human. Why don't I get a small group together for drinks after work? You could join us and meet a few more of your co-workers."

"Oh." Andi couldn't believe how easy this was. "I'd like that, but I already have a commitment after work today." She felt Maggie pull back and knew the woman thought she'd made up an excuse not to go out with her. "Could-could we do it another day this week instead? I'd really like to meet more people."

Maggie smiled. "Of course. How about Wednesday? Sloppy's Sports Bar has a Wednesday Happy Hour with excellent munchies."

"Great!" Andi had no idea what type of place Sloppy's was and she didn't care. "I'd love to join you. Should I meet you there or what?" She didn't want to walk into a strange bar by herself but if it meant she might make a friend or two she could do it.

"Nah. We'll all walk over together from here. It keeps the guys from hitting on us if we're in a group. I'll let you know when we're ready to go. We usually head out right after work."

Two lights on Maggie's console began to blink. "Gotta get back to this." She picked up her headset and slid it over her hair.

Andi gave a little wave and continued on to her office. It wasn't until she sat down to her computer and saw her reflection in the monitor that she realized she was smiling.

Last night she had stood up to her mother. Today she had taken the first step toward getting to know her co-workers. And tonight she had a dinner date with a man who interested her and made her pulse race.

The smile stayed with her all day, until her father's administrative assistant called down late afternoon and told her Cepheus requested her immediate presence in his office.

For the briefest of moments Andi considered not answering her father's summons, but she knew that he would show up at her office door if she didn't go to him and she didn't want to provide a scene for her co-workers.

He most likely wanted to scold her for the way she'd walked out last night. Or for the way she'd spoken to her mother. Cass would have relayed their conversation to her father verbatim. Or he wanted to scold her for refusing to have dinner with that creep Angus Ames. Whichever one it turned out to be she felt fairly confident that it involved a lecture. Like her mother Cepheus White was an expert lecturer, at least when it came to his only child.

Andi walked into her father's outer office ten minutes later. She had taken the time to wrap up and save the spreadsheet she was working on. Depending on how upset her father was his lectures could go on for a while. A long while.

She smelled coffee and the faint aroma of leather along with the fresh green of the large plants an outside company regularly maintained and rotated for the office.

The top floor of the Cepheus White building was a show-case for visiting sports figures and her father's various business partners. The deep blue carpet was thick and cushy underfoot, the waiting room furnished with large leather seats to accommodate the often larger than average athletes. A carved black walnut buffet set against one wall offered top grade coffee, teas, or cold drinks from its camouflaged refrigerator unit.

Windows looked out over the river and La Crosse's historic district. The atmosphere was an almost reverential hush, with the sales force handling deals in quiet voices behind mostly closed office doors.

"Hi Spencer. Should I go right in?" Her father's admin Spencer, a whip-thin, middle-aged man who always struck her as stiff and formal, stood to escort her to her father's door just as she'd known he would.

"Good afternoon, Miss White. I'll just see you to the door and let Mr. White know you're here." His reedy voice sounded faintly disapproving. Andi couldn't recall the admin ever speaking to her in any other tone but a disapproving one.

"Of course. Thank you, Spencer. Do you know why my father wants to see me?"

"I'm sure I don't, Miss."

*And you wouldn't tell me if you did,* thought Andi as she followed the admin's narrow back.

Her father's office was the largest and grandest of all. Set in the southeast corner of the building, it boasted two walls of floor to ceiling windows. Spencer announced her and backed out, closing the heavy carved door behind him. Andi stepped over to her favorite view and watched a tug push one of the large flotillas of barges that carried grain down the river.

The men and women who handled the tugs never failed to impress her. Six barges were connected, two wide and three long, into flotillas that were longer than three football fields and carried more than nine thousand tons of grain. A single tug maneuvered the unwieldy load through narrow locks day and night, a feat that took confidence, steady hands, and calm nerves.

Reluctantly, Andi turned away from the activity on the river. "You wanted to see me, Dad?"

Her father sat behind his desk, a wide expanse of

mahogany covered with neat piles of forms and two large monitors. She knew he was displeased by the way she had ignored him and walked to the windows but she'd needed a minute when she saw him behind the desk.

Usually her father invited her to join him in his seating area near the windows, a collection of four old leather club chairs with a heavy glass coffee table set in the middle of the group. Whenever she'd visited his office growing up they'd sit there and talk, usually with a cold lemonade or other age appropriate refreshment.

By remaining behind his desk her father was letting her know that whatever this meeting was about it was serious. She took one of the two hard mahogany chairs in front of the desk and waited.

"Your mother and I were less than pleased by your behavior last night," he began.

"I know, Dad, but–" He held up a hand to stop her from speaking.

"Let me finish. You insulted a man who is very important to our company. Angus Ames is a key supplier and we work hard to keep him happy. I would like to hear the reason why you behaved the way you did. A *good* reason why." He sat back in his large black leather desk chair and waited, his eyes never wavering from Andi's face.

She took a deep breath and let it out. "The simple truth is that I don't like Angus Ames and I don't want to have dinner with him."

Cepheus leaned forward and placed his elbows on his desk. He steepled his fingers and tapped his forefingers together. Andi knew that that gesture generally meant she wasn't going to like what followed.

"Your mother and I have sacrificed and worked hard to make Cepheus White Sports what it is today," he began.

Andi wanted to squirm in her seat. She had heard this speech before.

"And one thing we learned early on is that sometimes we have to deal with people we don't necessarily like. Whether we like them or not they still deserve to be treated with respect. There's nothing wrong with Angus Ames. He's a successful businessman with a good reputation."

"There's nothing wrong with him except that he wants get into my pants," Andi blurted out, "and I don't want to sleep with him."

"Andi!" Her father's face reddened. "That's enough of that kind of talk. My point is that I won't have you walking out on a guest in our home or rudely talking back to your mother like you did last night."

Anger propelled Andi to her feet. She placed her palms flat on the desk and looked down at her father.

"That's right. Angus Ames was a guest in *your* home, not mine. I attend all of your company functions at *your* bidding–even though I'm not interested–because I want to please you. I let you parade me in front of your colleagues and the athletes you're hoping to sign on. I put up with strangers and lecherous men touching me when I really want to swat their hands away because Mother says I must.

"Why do those men come before me, Dad? Why aren't you protecting me instead of-of . . . " Charles's words came to her. "-*pimping* me out?"

Tears sprang to her eyes. She furiously dashed them away, angry at the sign of weakness. Jerking back from the desk she began to pace the floor.

"I hate those functions. I'm not like you and Mother."

"I didn't realize you felt that way." Her father's words were stiff. "We assumed you were interested in helping us build the company."

Andi whirled to face him. "Why would you think that? How many job interviews did you sabotage for me before I was finally forced to give in and work here? Didn't it occur to you that I wanted to make something of myself on my own? Did it ever occur to you that I wanted to be someone other than Cepheus White's b-beautiful daughter and shown off like some-some . . . object?"

"What's wrong with being my beautiful daughter?" Cepheus stood and pointed a finger at her face. "You *are* beautiful, incredibly beautiful. You should feel proud that you turn heads wherever you go."

Her anger drained away and she hugged herself, suddenly cold. Her father didn't understand and she didn't know how to make him understand. "Why should I feel proud, Dad? I didn't make myself beautiful. I had nothing to do with my face or the way I'm built. They're an accident of birth. I'd much rather be admired for something I did than how I look."

"Don't talk like that. Your beauty is a gift. Your mother has worked hard to teach you how to use it."

Andi felt like she had at school when the other girls invariably grew jealous of her and turned against her. She felt wrapped in cotton wool, observing her surroundings through a thick film. Separate. An observer and never a full participant.

"Was there anything else?" she asked quietly.

"Yes. We covered for you last night. Your mother told Angus that you were taken ill. Angus is insisting that he get the chance to take you out to dinner. Your mother assured him that you would be free this coming Friday night. He'll pick you up at seven."

"And if I refuse?"

"You won't like the consequences."

"What are you saying?" She fisted her hands to stop their trembling.

"I hold the mortgages on the building your condo is in."

A wave of nausea washed through her and she staggered slightly. She couldn't believe what her father was threatening. "What?" She shook her head. "No, you can't. I bought the condo through First Trust Bank. They hold my mortgage."

"They did hold it. Then they sold the mortgages in the secondary mortgage market."

A sense of inevitability filled Andi. She couldn't win against her parents. She would never be anything but their pawn, a piece to manipulate as they saw fit.

"What are you saying? Spell it out, Dad." She had to ask. She needed to hear her father say just how far he was willing to go to force his daughter to bend to his will.

"I'm saying that Angus Ames is critical to my company's survival. If having dinner with my daughter makes the man happy then that's what he gets. Make no mistake, Andromeda, if I have to call in your mortgage in order to get you to have dinner with Angus, I will."

Andi couldn't believe her ears. "You'd turn me out of my home."

"In a word, yes. Although I'd hate for it to come to that. This Friday, Andromeda. Angus will pick you up at seven. You may go."

Feeling shell-shocked and betrayed, Andi turned and left her father's office.

# CHAPTER 10

IT WAS seven o'clock Monday evening and Andi was still lying on her couch hugging a pillow and staring out the window. The view, always captivating and soothing, barely registered on her brain.

She had left her father's office and taken the stairs past the seventh floor, not counting the steps for perhaps the first time in her life. She didn't bother to return to her own office. All she could think of was escape.

Fortunately she had grabbed her tote when she went to the eighth floor to see her father so she had it with her. She had left her office unlocked but she didn't care. She had needed to get out of the building as quickly as possible. Needed to get away before she fell apart.

She felt gutted, angry. Hollowed out. And so alone. So very, very lonely. She had no girlfriend to call and vent on, no friend of any gender to help her figure out what to do next. Her mother would side with her father. Charles would defend her but it would put his job at risk and she could never do that to him.

She tossed the pillow she held to the floor. Spook arched

his back and hissed at it, the short hairs on his tail fluffed like a miniature bottle brush.

Even though her parents had sent her to a girl's boarding school as soon as she was old enough she'd always believed they loved her in their own way. Now she wasn't so sure. Her father had made it painfully clear to her that his company came first in their hearts, leaving little room for a daughter. She was just another tool for them to use as they saw fit.

She had tried so hard to please them over the years, always the dutiful daughter doing what she could to contribute to the success of Cepheus White Sports. For what? Her parents just kept asking her for more. The one time she had said no and look what happened. They expected her to compromise her integrity to keep a business associate like Angus Ames happy. She felt like one of their trophies handed from winning team to winning team.

She was so sick of feeling sorry for herself but she didn't know what to *do*.

The buzzer connected to the downstairs door made her start but she made no effort to answer it. It was probably her mother, here to back up her father.

She definitely did not want to see her mother. Two minutes later she heard a knock at her door. Cass must have buzzed all the condos until someone let her into the building. Let her knock. Andi had no intention of answering.

"Andi? You in there?"

Not her mother. The voice was deep. Perseus. She'd forgotten all about their dinner date.

She didn't want to see him either.

"Andi? I know you're in there. If you changed your mind about dinner that's fine. At least take these flowers I brought you. Then I'll leave you alone."

Andi let another minute pass. Perseus knocked again. "I'll just leave them here by the door, okay? I'm leaving now."

Flowers. Percy had brought her flowers.

She leaped off the couch and ran to the door. "Percy, wait!" She didn't see anyone through the security peephole. She was too late. What an idiot. She should have at least thanked him and made an excuse for forgetting to cancel their date.

She undid all the locks and pulled open the door. A large bouquet of deep blue orchids sat on her doormat. "Oh. Oh, they're beautiful." Tears flowed freely down her cheeks. And here she'd thought she was all cried out.

"They match your eyes."

Andi's head whipped to her right. Perseus was leaning with one shoulder against the wall, his hands in his pockets. He was wearing dark dress slacks and a sage green shirt that intensified the green of his eyes.

He was looking her over carefully. She could see his body tense when he realized something bad had happened to her but he talked about the flowers instead of grilling her.

"They're called Ocean Breeze orchids," he said easily. "I was looking for yellow roses but as soon as I saw the orchids they made me think of you. Their deep blue, almost violet color matches your beautiful eyes."

He reached out and gently wiped the tears from her left cheek with his thumb. "I don't think the flowers are the only reason you're crying."

He looked pointedly at her running shorts and tee shirt and bare feet. "And something tells me you forgot all about our dinner date. I'm wounded."

Andi brought the bouquet to her face and inhaled their subtle spicy scent. "I need to put these in water. Please come in."

Perseus relaxed slightly and followed Andi inside. He had no intention of leaving until he learned what or who had distressed her so badly.

"Wow." He stopped in front of the windows. "Fantastic view. This is where I'd hang out if I had this place. I love a water view no matter what the body of water. Ocean, lake, river–even ponds are interesting."

His voice followed her into the kitchen area where she found a clear, hand-blown vase that her mother had given her. She filled the vase, put in the flower food and bouquet, and set them on the black granite island that separated the kitchen from the living area.

"Thank you, Percy. The flowers are incredibly beautiful." She remained behind the island, suddenly uncomfortable with his presence. Even though she'd lived there two years Percy was the first visitor to her condo other than her parents and she wasn't sure how she should act.

"I'm sorry about dinner. I clean forgot. To be honest I don't feel much like going out tonight. Sorry," she said again.

"It's all right, Andi. No need to apologize. Obviously something important to you has upset you. I think we still need to eat though. Do you have a favorite pizza place that delivers? We'll order a pie or two and eat in."

"I–" Andi stopped. She'd been about to tell Percy she needed to be alone. To do what? Wallow some more in self-pity? She'd been feeling sorry for herself because she didn't have anyone to talk to and here was a decent man who had brought her beautiful flowers because they reminded him of her.

On top of that he was willing to eat pizza instead of the dinner out he had planned. With no complaints. Just how big a fool was she?

"Yes, I have a favorite pizza place," she told him. "What do you like on yours? I'll call and order. You can buy."

"Deal. I'll take a medium pizza with the works. Do you have beer or wine here?"

"Wine, no beer. I rarely drink beer."

"Wine's fine."

Forty minutes later they were seated side by side at the island eating and talking. Perseus knew she had been uncomfortable with him when he first arrived. And he knew that something had wounded her deeply. While she had relaxed a great deal since his arrival he could still see the pain in her eyes.

He allowed her to direct the conversation wherever she chose, occasionally asking a question or two, subtly probing to narrow down the problem.

After they'd eaten and cleaned up the mess they retired to the couch with fresh glasses of wine. Andi's adorable kitten Spook climbed up his pant leg and curled up on his lap. They sat in a companionable silence as twilight descended on the city and lights began to glow on the river.

"Would you like to tell me what happened today?" he asked. "I know it had to be bad. You're normally a very composed and together woman. It would take a lot to shake you. Has someone close to you died?"

Andi shook her head. "No. Well, maybe. In a way yes."

"Hmmm. No, maybe, yes. Is that a multiple choice answer?" He cradled Spook's back with his palm, feeling each tiny knob of the kitten's spine. Such a delicate, vulnerable little creature. The kitten had been lucky when Andi found him. Most people would have either ignored the bag or left him there once they saw what was in it.

Andi watched Percy handle the kitten. He was a big man who was capable of great gentleness. He'd been terrific with the children at Zee and Pandora's house and they obviously adored him. Even Samantha's children called him Uncle Percy.

She felt the pressure behind her eyes that told her it would be easy to start crying again. She pushed back on it and focused on Spook.

"My parents had me over for dinner last night. Do you remember the older blonde man who asked me to dinner at Friday night's event–Angus Ames? You saved me from having to go out with him."

She frowned at him suddenly. "I never thought to ask–why did you do that? You didn't even know me then."

Percy's green eyes were steady on hers. "I was on my way to introduce myself to you. I saw the way you pulled away from his hand when he touched your bare back. And when you smiled at him your eyes didn't smile. I figured you weren't crazy about the guy and could use a little help."

"I see." To her knowledge no one had ever noticed that her smiles rarely reached her eyes. She found it a little unsettling that Percy saw so much about her. She sipped her wine to give herself time to collect her thoughts before continuing.

"So anyway, Sunday night I showed up at my parents' house for what I thought was a family dinner and Angus Ames was there."

"Ames was stalking you?"

"No. He'd been invited. Mr. Ames is an important supplier to my father's company and my parents wanted to give him another chance to ask me out."

"Did they know you didn't want to see Ames socially?"

"No, but it wouldn't have mattered anyway." Now came the first of the hard parts. Andi cleared her throat. "Mr. Ames asked me to have dinner with him tonight in front of my parents and I said no, I had made plans. He didn't take it well."

"I hope your parents showed Ames the door."

When Andi didn't say anything for a long moment he swore softly. "I think I'm beginning to understand. Your parents want you to have dinner with Ames regardless of how you feel about it, don't they?"

Andi jerked her head in an abrupt nod. "My mother and I had words and I left. Today I accused my father of acting like a pimp."

"Well hell, Andi, he is. I don't blame you for being upset."

"That wasn't the end of it, unfortunately."

"You're kidding. There's more?"

"Today my father told me he'd demand full payment on the mortgage for my condo unless I have dinner with Mr. Ames on Friday night." To her embarrassment she felt tears slide down her cheeks.

Percy's jaw hardened. "Jeezus. Your old man would do that to you? That's . . . that's just vile." He set his wineglass on the low pine coffee table and set Spook on the arm of the couch.

Before she realized his intention he'd scooped her up and set her on his lap, pulling her close to his chest and wrapping his arms around her. She struggled against him even though what she wanted more than anything was to snuggle closer.

"I'm too big. You can't hold me in your lap," she whispered.

"Nonsense. You fit perfectly."

Andi knew she was a big woman. Not big as in overweight but big as in tall. Statuesque. Being picked up as if she was a child and set on Percy's lap left her feeling flustered and a little breathless. She liked it.

No. The truth was, she loved it.

# CHAPTER 11

"I'm sorry your parents are trying to back you into a corner." Percy's large hands rubbed Andi's back and arm in long, soothing strokes that made her want to melt into him.

With her ear against Percy's chest she could hear it rumble when he spoke. He smelled of a subtle musky spice and fresh air and he felt big and warm and strong. She felt safe, safer than she'd felt in a long time. Maybe even ever.

She couldn't remember her father ever holding her in his lap like this and wondered if he ever had. Somehow she doubted it. If anyone had ever held her to comfort her it would have been her father's driver/handyman Charles.

She didn't want Perseus to think she was weak even though at the moment she *felt* weak.

"You didn't do anything to feel sorry about," she told him. Her voice sounded a little weak but at least it was steady. "I'm upset because today I learned that my father's company is more important to my parents than my happiness. I don't like Angus Ames. I certainly don't want to have dinner with him. Worse, I have a feeling he's looking for more than dinner. I think he wants to nail Cepheus White's virgin daughter."

She felt Percy's body still and stiffen beneath her. "Crap. Sorry. I probably shouldn't have said that. Too much information, right? Forget that last bit." What had happened to her natural reserve? It seemed to have flown out the window when Perseus pulled her onto his lap.

Percy chuckled. His arms tightened around her. "I guess that really would make your father a pimp, wouldn't it?"

Andi couldn't help herself. In spite of how bad she felt she grinned briefly at the thought of her father being labeled a pimp, then deflated again. "I'm screwed. I either get to have dinner and wrestle with a man I detest or I lose my home. I'll tell you one thing, if I'm ever blessed with children I will always put them first."

Percy tilted his head back so he could see her face. "Why did you take out a mortgage from your father? Was it a money thing? You couldn't get a regular bank mortgage?"

She shook her head. The action rubbed her cheek against Percy's strong pectoral muscle. Now that she was aware of it she realized his entire body was hard, powerful muscle. She'd never been this close to a man before. It made her feel a little tingly and disoriented.

She forced herself to focus on the conversation before she did something foolish like bury her nose in the triangle of golden chest hair peeking through the vee of Percy's shirt.

"I was able to get a mortgage. I signed one with First Trust Bank because I wanted to buy the condo on my own without my parents' help. Somehow Dad must have tracked it down and bought all the mortgages for this building on the secondary mortgage market. All he has to do is dangle Super Bowl tickets or dinner with a famous athlete in front of someone and he pretty much gets whatever he wants."

"I see. Too bad. I'm afraid we can't do much about that now. Unless you have the money to pay off the mortgage?" He looked down at her. She seemed calmer now that she'd shared her problem with him, but he wanted her to get her mad on and get rid of the shadows that still lurked in the back of her beautiful eyes.

Andi's parents had made her feel weak and unsure of herself. The fact that Cepheus and Cass White would treat the majestic woman who was their daughter like a commodity to be bought and sold angered Perseus beyond words.

"Unfortunately, no, I can't pay off the mortgage," Andi told him, "but you don't have to worry about me. I'll figure out something. Thanks for listening. I feel a little better now. You don't have to hold me anymore."

As soon as she said the words she knew she wasn't ready to leave the warm comfort of his body.

"I'm not holding you because I feel I have to, Andi. I'm holding you because I want to. I also want to help you."

Andi tilted her head back against his shoulder and looked up at him. "*Why* are you helping me? First at the function Friday night and now today. You barely know me. Why are you being so nice to me?"

He smiled at her, his eyes crinkling at the corner. A dimple appeared in his left cheek. Andi's heart did a little flip and her breath caught. She wanted to plant a kiss on that dimple.

"Maybe I'm hoping to score a couple Super Bowl tickets," he teased.

She smiled back. "Somehow I doubt that."

"Isn't it obvious?" His gaze dropped to her full lips. He hesitated a moment before brushing his mouth lightly over hers. "I like you." He kissed her again, still soft and sweet and brief but a real kiss.

"And I want to get to know you better."

His mouth was only inches from hers. Andi's breath caught again when he moved in and touched his lips to hers, more firmly this time. His lips felt soft yet demanding on hers and the kiss began to fill those hollowed out spots deep inside her body. She wrapped her left arm around his neck and wound her fingers in silky black hair. His heart thudded beneath her ear.

She tried to push closer. Needed to get closer. Percy groaned and gently pried her lips apart with his tongue. She stilled for a moment, shocked at the intimacy of having a man's tongue in her mouth, then sucked on it tentatively.

The result was electrifying. And not at all what she expected.

Perseus stood abruptly and set her away from him on the couch. He ran a hand through his hair and over his face. He was breathing hard and his face was flushed under his tan.

He didn't want to stop kissing Andromeda White. He wanted to kiss every inch of her glorious body. He wanted to bury himself deep inside her.

And there was the problem. Only a few minutes before she'd confessed to being a virgin. He'd almost forgotten.

He hated the way she was looking at him. Bewildered and hurt and not a little embarrassed. He hated that he had put that look on her face.

"What?"Andi crossed her arms over her chest. " What did I do wrong?"

"Not a damn thing." He dropped his hand and took a deep breath.

Andi watched his chest rise and fall and wished he still held her against it. She'd liked being held on Percy's lap.

She'd especially enjoyed his kiss. What had she done to get such a reaction?

"I must have done something wrong," she insisted. "You were kissing me and then you . . . weren't. Something made you stop. I didn't want you to stop." She couldn't believe she was admitting those things to the man in front of her but she needed to know why he didn't want her.

"You didn't do anything wrong," he said again. "But–"

"But what?" Anger was beginning to replace Andi's embarrassment. She frowned up at him.

Perseus lifted his hands and let them drop. "You're a virgin. An innocent. You don't understand what could have happened here. I'm not the kind of man who takes advantage of a woman when she's vulnerable."

Andi shot to her feet and poked a finger in Percy's chest. His large, very firm chest distracted her. She wanted to run her palms over it. She wanted to see what he looked like without a shirt. Funny, she'd seen plenty of shirtless athletes but none of them had ever interested her the way Percy's body did. With a great deal of effort she pulled her thoughts back to the conversation.

"You act like my virginity is some type of disease."

"*What?* Don't be daft. That's not it at all." The subject made him uncomfortable. He tended to get testy when he felt uncomfortable. All the Olympic gods did. And when they got testy things happened. Terrible things like lightning storms and earthquakes and such. Even a demigod like Perseus could cause a small disaster.

Andi was scowling and still poking him in the chest. He grabbed her wrist and held it so she couldn't poke him any more.

The scowl changed to a glare. "You just said I was a virgin and therefore vulnerable." She tried to pull her hand free and clenched her jaw when she couldn't. He had such strong hands. What would those hands feel like on her bare skin?

*Focus, Andi,* she told herself. *Now is not the time to be thinking about losing your virginity.* Except that it was. In fact it was well past time. She was tired of lugging the label of virgin around with her.

"Andi, listen to me. You're vulnerable because you're upset over what your family is trying to do to you. Not because you're a virgin. Dammit. Don't twist my words."

"I didn't twist your words. And I'm not an idiot. I know about sex. I read." Frustrated that Perseus so easily held her captive, Andi stamped her foot and went back to scowling at him.

"I–I don't even know what to say to that." She'd gotten her mad on like he wanted, only he hadn't planned on the mad being directed at him. Despite that, there was a part of him that was fascinated and not a little turned on by her anger. Who knew the cool, composed woman he'd met Friday night could get so fired up? Would she show that kind of passion in bed?

Sensing his distraction, Andi yanked her hand free. She stalked to her door and opened it. "I think it's time for you to go," she told him, hands on hips.

Percy stared at her for a minute before heading for the door. She was without a doubt the most beautiful woman he'd ever met. And feisty. He liked that.

"You're right. It's time for me to leave. Good night, Andi."

He started toward the stairs but turned abruptly and was back in the doorway in two long strides. Grabbing Andi by the upper arms he pulled her to him and kissed her until he felt her soften. When she moaned and leaned into him he released her.

"I'll call you." He headed back toward the stairs without a backward glance.

Andi slammed the door behind him. What had that last kiss been about? She put her fingers to her still tingling lips.

Crap. She didn't want Percy to leave, not really. She wanted him to kiss her again. She wanted to see where the kissing led. If the effect Percy's kisses had on her body was any indication she had a feeling she would like it.

Unfortunately the man had something against virgins. Her and her big mouth. Why did she have to tell him? She certainly hadn't intended to. It had just popped out. Of course at the time she'd had no idea the man was interested in kissing her. She could chalk that little oversight up to her lack of experience.

She banged her head softly against the door in frustration.

Perseus trotted down the stairs with a scowl on his face. What the hell had happened to his control back there? He was holding Andi to comfort her and get her to talk about her problem and then–and then he couldn't resist kissing her.

She had fit on his lap like she was made for him and that beautiful mouth of hers had been only inches away. He'd been weak. He'd succumbed to temptation. And once he had kissed her he had needed more.

He ignored the little voice that told him he would always need more of Andromeda White.

Damn. She'd tasted a little of wine, a little of pizza sauce, and a whole lot of sweet that was uniquely Andi. Just thinking about the kiss made his abdomen tighten.

Crap. He wasn't the kind of guy who took advantage of vulnerable women, and Andromeda was a vulnerable woman if ever he met one–at least tonight she was. He'd done the honorable thing. The right thing. She was just too innocent to realize he had acted in her best interest.

He couldn't believe a woman as beautiful as Andromeda was still a virgin at twenty-four. Most women he knew experimented with sex in college, sometimes even high school. What would have happened if she hadn't told him she had no experience?

He knew the answer to that. They'd be tangled in her bed sheets even now.

He stepped out into the warm evening and stood on the sidewalk. Part of him—a very large part of him—wanted to turn around and storm back into Andi's condo, take her into his arms and make love to her. He wanted to finish what they'd started.

He sighed deeply and swore. Andi needed time. Time to process everything that had happened to her today—and that included his kisses.

Andi had responded to him in a way that was very gratifying to his ego. He'd watched those deep blue eyes of hers blur with desire. He fully intended to make them blur again. But not tonight. She needed to deal with the pain of her parents' betrayal and find her footing again.

In the meanwhile he would be her friend and try to help her. Only then would he pursue his goal of becoming her lover.

Perseus set off toward where he'd left his car, unaware that he was being watched.

ANDI ALMOST CALLED in sick Tuesday because she didn't want to see her father but decided it would be a cowardly thing to do. She needn't have worried. Her father made no effort to speak with her again that day or the next. Neither did her mother. Apparently they felt that they'd said all there was to say and they expected her to have dinner with Angus Ames on Friday.

She wasn't sure what angered her more–that her parents assumed she would do as she was told or that they didn't feel the need to extract a promise from her that she would have dinner with Angus Ames. That they felt they could tell her to do something as if she was still a child and then expected her to obey without question.

She brooded over it all day while she crunched numbers.

"Andi, are you ready?" Maggie stood in the doorway to Andi's office with a huge red handbag hanging off her shoulder. Carrot colored curls bounced in a wild disarray around her freckled face. Her full breasts sat high in a turquoise scoop-necked tank top. A matching mini skirt barely covered tanned, freckled legs. Maggie looked like Andi's memories of summer camp, not an office worker.

Andi frowned at her, perplexed. She hadn't spoken to Maggie since Monday morning and had no idea what the customer service rep was talking about. "Am I ready for what?"

Now it was Maggie's turn to frown. "We're having drinks at Sloppy's, remember? Four of the other girls are joining us."

"Oh!" She'd forgotten all about the plan she had made Monday to go out with a few of the customer service reps after work. That conversation seemed like a lifetime ago. Before her life had imploded.

"I'm really sorry, Maggie, but I don't think I can–"

Maggie wouldn't let her finish. "You work too hard, Andi. You're usually here before anyone else and you're the last one to leave. I thought you wanted to meet some of your co-workers. Or were you just being nice to a lowly customer service rep?"

The comment stung. Andi remembered how friendly Maggie had been towards her on Monday. "No, I wasn't stringing you along. I really would like to meet some of the others and have a drink."

"Come on, then. Sloppy's Happy Hour just started. We need to get there and grab a good table. Magalicious munchies await."

"Just let me shut this down. I'll be right there."

It felt strange riding the elevator to the ground floor with five other women, all chattering away. It made Andi wonder if she had started using the stairs to avoid having to talk to anyone. She'd told herself it was for the exercise, but she suspected it was at least partly to avoid other people.

She felt the strangest urge to giggle at the shock on Gus's

face when he saw her step off the elevator with the other women. "Goodnight, Gus."

A wide smile split the old man's wrinkled face. "Good night, Miss Andromeda. Sure am glad to see you getting out of here at a decent hour."

Sloppy's sat two blocks from the office and was a revelation in how the average working girl could afford to go out. The group of women Maggie had invited to join them were friendly and talkative. They had all refreshed their make-up and hair before leaving the office. One had changed into a halter top covered with sparkling sequins.

They piled into Sloppy's with gleams in their eyes and smiles on their faces, keeping Andi in the middle of the group. She had the feeling they were expecting her to turn tail and run.

"Just until you learn the ropes." Lauren, a tall blonde Norwegian, must have read her mind. Lauren was the spangled halter top wearer. She had paired hers with tight, low slung jeans and sported a fake ruby in her navel.

At least Andi assumed it was fake. She thought Lauren looked confident and sexy as hell.

Lauren inspected Andi's conservative linen suit and shook her head. "Next time remember to bring a more Sloppy's-appropriate outfit to change into."

The bar was already over half full with more coming through the door behind them. Maggie commandeered a large round table in the middle of the long, open bar.

"Wouldn't you rather take that table over there?" Andi asked, pointing to a similar table set discreetly in the corner.

"Nope. Trust us. This is right where we need to be. We're lucky to snag it."

Andi took a seat between Lauren and Maggie and looked around her. She was relieved to see that despite its name

Sloppy's was a clean bar. It took up most of the ground floor of a historic brick building set on a corner. Large picture windows looking onto the two streets let in plenty of light and offered a chance to watch passersby.

The original oak floor boards had been refinished and glossed with easy care polyurethane, the ductwork and ceiling overhead painted a dull black. It smelled of beer and perfume, popcorn and barbecue.

High counters with tall stools lined both walls of windows. A long, dark bar with a brass foot rail ran the entire length of the right side of the room. A portion of the brick wall behind it was mirrored, reflecting what looked like hundreds of bottles of colored liquors.

High top wooden tables lined the back wall with a mix of round and square tables filling the remainder of the floor. Large flat screen televisions were strategically placed so every seat could view several and presumably watch which-ever game interested them. Andi saw tennis, baseball, and soccer games in progress.

There were none of the green plants or hushed conversa-tion Andi was used to in the bars her parents used for busi-ness meetings. Sloppy's wasn't pretending to be anything other than what it was—a sports bar where people gathered to drink and flirt and watch games. Even only half full it was loud and boisterous and lively.

Andi guessed the place could easily hold several hundred people. The thought made her feel a little panicky. This wasn't one of her father's events where all she had to do was paste a smile on her face and make small talk.

"What'll it be today girls?" A buxom brunette snapped her gum and flung small paper drink napkins onto the table in front of each of them.

"Hi, Michelle. This is Andi White. This is her first time

here." Lauren ordered a Slippery Nipple. Everyone ordered an exotic cocktail except for Andi who asked for a glass of white wine.

"You have to loosen up, Andi," Lauren told her. "You can have wine anytime. The cocktails are half price here on Wednesdays."

"Oh, well, maybe I'll try one later." Andi wanted to fit in with the other women but she never drank anything stronger than beer or wine and only small amounts of those. As soon as she'd grown up enough to ask about alcohol her mother had drilled into her that ladies didn't get drunk.

"Don't worry," a petite dark-haired girl said. "We never have to pay for anything after our first round of drinks."

Andi's brow furrowed. She didn't understand what Ashley–at least she thought her name was Ashley–was telling her. "Why not? Surely the owners can't afford to give away alcohol. That's where bars and most restaurants make all their money."

"Watch and learn, honey," Ashley told her. She sipped her cocktail and smacked her lips. "Yum. Watch and learn. We have this down to a science."

She wasn't lying, Andi realized an hour later. The women flirted and smiled and soon the table was covered with empty and full drink glasses. Maggie had talked Andi into switching to mojitos and they were slipping down her throat far too easily. Ah, but they tasted so good. She was beginning to see why cocktails were a popular choice. And at half price she could drink twice as many!

A man sitting at the bar smiled at her. Pleasantly buzzed, she smiled back. A minute later Michelle slid another mojito in front of her and indicated the smiling man at the bar. "From Steve over there." She wandered off to take more orders.

Someone had turned up the music as the bar filled with the after work crowd. Men and women sat and stood and flirted between tables and talked and ate truly magalicious munchies. Groans and shouts told Andi some people were following the games on the tvs.

Glasses clinked and laughter rang out. Michelle and two other waitresses circulated through the crowd with trays filled with drinks and food or empty glasses held high over their heads.

Andi didn't know how the waitresses managed to move through the jostling crowd without dropping or spilling anything. It was like a dance. "I love this place," she said suddenly.

"Yeah, it rocks." Lauren raised a glass and they toasted each other with a loud clink. "Especially on Wednesdays."

"Andromeda, darling. What a surprise to see you here."

Andi turned at the familiar masculine voice. "André! What are you doing here?" She stood and kissed him on the cheek.

"I usually stop by Sloppy's when I'm in town. I find it's good for my ego." He hugged her and winked at the others.

"André, these are my co-workers." She introduced him to the other women who were all wide-eyed and slack jawed, staring at the handsome soccer player as if he was God come to visit. André made small talk with them for a few minutes then excused himself, kissing Andi's cheek when he left.

Andi sat back down and picked up her drink. It took her a few seconds to realize the table was quiet and all the women were staring at her.

"What? Do I have food in my teeth?"

"André Lightfoot kissed your cheek. He *hugged* you. I think I'm going to swoon," Maggie said. "How do you happen to know André Lightfoot? Tell us. Inquiring minds demand to know." All five women leaned toward Andi.

She lifted one shoulder in a half shrug. "I met him at one of my father's parties a couple years ago." Thinking about her father made her scowl. "I hate going to them but my parents insist."

Her lips felt a little numb when she talked. What a strange feeling. She rolled them inward and then pursed them. Still numb.

"I can't believe you're complaining about getting to dress up and go to fancy parties and meet important people. What's to hate?" Ashley gave Andi a puzzled look.

Andi had noticed Ashley eyeing one particular guy leaning back on the bar for the last half hour. Dressed in faded jeans and a tee shirt stretched across impressive biceps, Andi had noticed his posing earlier and dismissed him as a vain body builder. To each their own. She took another sip of her drink. There was nothing wrong with muscles, she thought, thinking about Perseus. But not when they were overdone.

Maggie tapped Andi's hand to regain her attention. "Pay attention here, girl. Ashley asked you a question. What's to hate about your father's parties?"

"They're boring." Andi searched for a way to explain. Her words were slightly slurred, she realized. Funny, her tongue felt a little thick in her mouth. Was she drunk?

Yeah, she thought maybe she was. How about that? She smiled and made an effort to enunciate more clearly. "The parties—Dad calls them 'events'—are always the same. I stand around making small talk with people who are mostly shorter than I am and pretend I'm having a good time. *And* I always have to be nice to the businessmen and athletes whether I like them or not."

Five sets of eyes remained glued on her.

"Athletes?" Lauren repeated. Her pale blue eyes were gleaming.

Andi nodded. "Sure. Lots of athletes. Like André. There are always a few at Dad's parties."

"Who else have you met?" Ashley leaned forward, the body builder momentarily forgotten.

"Well . . ." Andi named a a quarterback who'd won two Super Bowl rings, and a pitcher she'd met recently. A tennis star. None of whom had impressed her. They had all been more interested in preening in front of the other guests and photographers than they had been in holding any kind of meaningful conversation. Although to be fair, that's why they were there.

"Who else? I can't believe you get to meet all those hot athletes." Ashley looked envious.

"Let's see . . " Andi named a few more. "My favorite is André though. He might be the only one I really talk to. He's charming and pleasant and makes me laugh poking fun at others. But not in a mean way," she added hastily. "He's really nice. He comes to Dad's events at least a couple times a year and makes a point to speak with me. Some of the athletes are so stuck on themselves that they're boring to talk to but André is interesting."

"Lightfoot is so hot," Maggie said. "I can't believe he comes to Sloppy's. I've never seen him here before. *And* we got to meet him thanks to you. He has great legs and a yummy ass. I just want to sink my teeth into it."

The other women groaned and agreed. The conversation veered toward athlete's with the hottest bodies.

Andi's jaw fell. She had never ever heard a female call a man's buttocks "yummy". She didn't know women talked about men that way. It seemed a little crude.

On the other hand, she had noticed that Perseus had a yummy ass. She could even picture herself nipping it. The thought made her smile until she remembered that she had tossed him out of her condo Monday night.

What a fool she was. She was going to end up being the city's oldest virgin if she kept on the way she was going.

Sloppy's no longer felt fun and welcoming. She wanted to go home and sober up. She stood, swayed a few moments, and plunked back down in her seat. Trying to walk home in heels with the world spinning was a bad idea. She slipped off her work shoes and tossed them into her tote without bothering to put them in their felt shoe bags.

*If only Mother could see me now.*

Andi slipped on her trainers and stood again. Much better. "I have to go," she told the others. "I have a kitten at home waiting for his dinner. Thank you for letting me join you. I had fun. And I hope I can come again sometime."

"You're always welcome," Maggie assured her.

Ashley's body builder had made his move and stood behind Ashley talking into her ear. Ashley lifted her hand in a goodbye wave but didn't take her attention off the man leaning over her.

Andi wondered if Ashley would take the body builder home with her or go to his place. Why was it so easy for other women to flirt with men but not for her?

Her brain was too muddled to figure it out at the moment so she let it go. She slung her tote strap over her shoulder and turned to leave but a hand on her arm stopped her.

"I'll walk you home," Lauren said, grabbing her own purse off the back of her chair. "You look a little wobbly. Besides, I want to hear more about the hunky men you've met."

There was only one man Andi thought hunky and she wasn't about to share him with the attractive Norwegian, but she welcomed the company. Truth was, she *did* feel a bit wobbly.

To her surprise Lauren turned out to be interesting and sharp-witted, the conversation easy. Andi found that she liked Lauren immensely and wondered if they might become friends. She invited Lauren up for a cup of coffee but Lauren declined. She had some studying to do, she told Andi. She taught part time at one of La Crosse's yoga studios and was going for her next level certification.

The women parted ways. Andi went upstairs to shower and sleep off the alcohol after feeding Spook.

Neither woman noticed that they were being watched.

# CHAPTER 13

ANDI SUFFERED her first ever hangover the next morning. She felt her pulse beating in her head, boom, boom, boom—a deep drumbeat of dull pain. She gulped several glasses of water in an effort to ease the dryness in her mouth but all they did was sit on her already bloated stomach. She felt like she had the flu without having the flu.

She was never going to touch another mojito as long as she lived. From now on no more hard liquor. She wasn't cut out to be a fun party girl. She was the contained, always in control, dull type of girl.

The glare of the morning sun made her recoil when she stepped outside her condo. She whimpered and fumbled in her tote for her sunglasses, crying a gasp of relief when she put them on. How did Maggie and the others do it?

The others had all drunk more than she had—she'd seen the evidence of their empty cocktail glasses on the table. Yet none of them had been as wobbly as she had been after only two, no three—wait, how many of those alcohol bombs did she drink? Four. Four mojitos.

Jeezus, she drank four mojitos. And they went down so easily.

Never again, she vowed. If Maggie invited her to another Sloppy's Happy Hour she would stick with her customary glass of white wine.

She wondered if Ashley had hooked up with the body builder guy. The women she'd gone out with last night knew about men. They knew how to flirt and talk and be attractive to members of the opposite sex.

Maybe she should tell the others about Perseus breaking off his kiss and ask for their advice about how to go about seducing him.

No. She shook her head and then wished she hadn't when the pounding increased. Perseus was too beautiful to share and she didn't want any more competition than she probably already had. Who knew how many women were chasing him back . . . where? Wherever his home was. She knew so little about him.

She joined a small group of office workers waiting at the corner to cross the busy street at the light and studied them behind the blessedly dark lenses of her sunglasses. She'd probably stood at that very light with some of the same people on other work day mornings and had never really paid attention to them before.

She recognized a couple faces but no one spoke. Every one of them was lost in their own thoughts just like she had been, maybe thinking about the work day ahead or maybe what happened the night before. Did any of them go to Sloppy's? Were any of them hung over?

The group crossed the street on the walk signal and split apart. Andi turned left. Her father's building took up the entire block but the employee entrance was around the next corner on a side street.

Most of the first floor of the Cepheus White building housed the retail arm of the company. She passed large plate glass windows displaying mannequins dressed in jackets, tee shirts, caps, sweatpants and pajamas, all in various team colors. Team logos decorated the clothing and just about every other item a person could want–from duffle bags to mouse pads. Sports memorabilia was a huge, very lucrative, and highly competitive business.

Andi turned the corner and let herself in double glass doors, greeting Tony, one of the night watchman, with a wave. She headed for the stairs but only made it to the third floor before she began to sweat and feel weak.

Why on earth did people drink if it made them feel like this? she wondered as she exited the stairwell and called the elevator. It was fun at the time but the after effects sucked.

The noise on the third floor added to her misery. Dozens of monogramming machines hammered behind her. Rolling laundry baskets sat on either side of the machine operators, filled with bundles of articles waiting to be decorated with a team name or logo.

The air was filled with dust motes despite the best air filtration system her father could buy. Everyone on the floor wore noise cancelling headphones to protect their hearing and masks to protect their lungs.

It had been a mistake to stop at this floor. She hadn't thought about how noisy it could be. The elevator was taking far too long. Andi wished her head would just implode and get it over with. Finally the elevator showed up with a ding she couldn't hear. She stepped inside, grateful that the car was empty, and pressed the button for the seventh floor before sagging against the back wall.

Maggie looked up as Andi walked by her cubicle and grinned. "You look a little worse for wear, Andi. Did you have too much fun at Sloppy's?" Her tone was sweet and teasing.

Andi scowled at her. "It's all your fault. You gave me that first mojito. I don't drink hard liquor and now I know why."

"Poor baby." Maggie's smile grew. "Hangover? I have just the thing." She pulled a bottle of ibuprofen from her oversized handbag and handed Andi a couple. "Take these. You'll feel better in no time."

"Thanks." Andi turned away then turned back. "And thanks for letting me tag along last night. I enjoyed myself despite the hangover this morning."

"You'll get used to it." Her call light blinked and Maggie waved Andi off.

"Don't bet on it," Andi muttered under her breath.

Two hours later she stared at the spreadsheet she was working on with little success. The ibuprofen Maggie had given her had mostly taken care of the headache but her brain still felt muzzy. Her windowless office seemed stuffy. She needed fresh air.

Maybe it was time to call it quits for the day. She never took off for sick days. Surely no one would mind if she took the remainder of the day off.

The thought of napping on her couch in the warm sunshine with Spook purring on her chest appealed to her. She shut down the spreadsheet she was working on. Grabbing her tote to change back into her sneakers for the walk home she was surprised to find that her sneakers were still on her feet.

A bubble of laughter escaped her mouth. She definitely had a muzzy brain.

Andi forced herself to take the stairs to the first floor. Going down was much easier than going up, she reasoned. Plus there was always the off chance she could run into her father or his admin Spencer–or any one of the senior account managers who worked on the eighth floor–in the elevator. All would be sure to mention to her father that they'd seen her leave.

She did not want to see her father.

When she stepped out of the stairwell into the lobby Gus was speaking with a pair of policemen. He brightened when he saw her.

"Miss Andromeda, these two detectives are asking about Ashley Burke. I told them she works on the seventh floor. You went out with her last night, didn't you?"

The detectives both zeroed in on Andi. The older of the two looked to be late middle age with receding brown hair that gave him a high forehead. He looked fit and trim even in his nondescript brown suit and studied Andi through sharp brown eyes that looked like they didn't miss much.

She suddenly wished she was wearing her heels so she'd have a height advantage.

The second detective looked to be about her own age. He was body builder big with a thick neck and a shaved, bullet-shaped head. The look he gave her told her he was mentally stripping off her clothes. She stiffened and glared at him before turning her attention back to the older detective.

"Is Ashley in trouble, detective?"

"You might say that," the younger man drawled. "She's dead."

Both Gus and Andi staggered back.

The older detective shot his partner an irritated look before taking Andi's elbow. "Come take a seat, miss. Andromeda is it? My name is Detective Lee. We have a couple questions for you if you don't mind."

He guided her to the waiting area and pressed her down

into one of the lobby's cushioned chairs. "Could you tell me your name first, please?"

"Andromeda White. I work here. Where is Ashley? She can't be dead." It couldn't be true. She'd seen Ashley alive and well and having fun just last night. How could she be dead?

"Did you know Miss Burke well?"

Andi shook her head. "No. I just met her last night. Some of the customer service reps were headed to Sloppy's for the Happy Hour and they invited me along. It was the first time I'd met any of them. Except Maggie. I met Maggie on Monday," she corrected. "Did Ashley have an accident?"

Apparently the detectives were only in the mood to ask questions, not to share information with her. The younger cop merely stared at her through hooded eyes. Trying to intimidate her?

"Could you give me the names of the other women with you last night?" Detective Lee asked.

Andi didn't know any of the women's last names other than Maggie Hoffman, she told them.

"Tell us exactly what you remember about the bar. Did you notice anyone watching Ashley? Anyone paying particular attention to her? Someone she might have had words with?"

"No. No one argued. Everyone was having fun." She pressed the heels of her palms into her eyes to push back the tears.

"Come on, *Miss* White." Detective Lee's partner broke in. "Everyone knows you office girls go to Sloppy's Happy Hour for cheap booze and to hook up. You might as well tell us the truth. You were trolling for men."

Andi dropped her hands and looked at the bull-necked detective. The man's attitude put her back up.

"Ashley was with us–," she began, looking at Detective

Lee and ignoring Bull Neck. She stopped. Ashley and the body builder had been eyeing each other most of the evening. Had she gone home with him? If she had and she was dead then . . .

"Ashley didn't have an accident, did she?" she asked Detective Lee. "Something awful happened to her." She stared at the older detective and waited for the truth. She could see that he didn't want to tell her. He ran his hand over his forehead and back over his remaining hair. Was that how he'd lost his hair?

"We are only beginning our investigation but there is some question as to the cause of Miss Burke's death. Her body was found in the river by a jogger in Riverside Park this morning. It looks like she drowned."

Ashley's body had been left near Andi's condo. Her stomach clenched and heaved. She jumped to her feet. "Excuse me, I'm going to be ill." The bull-necked detective grabbed her arm.

"Let her go," Detective Lee ordered.

Andi didn't look back. She ran across the lobby to the restrooms and made it just in time. Dabbing at her face and the back of her neck with a wet paper towel, she waited for her body to stop trembling before she returned to the detectives.

Detective Lee looked concerned, Bull Neck contemptuous. She ignored the younger detective and again focused on Lee.

"There was a man at the bar. He seemed interested in Ashley. Or rather, they seemed interested in each other. He looked like an overzealous body builder."

"How would you know?" Bull Neck demanded.

"He looked like you, like someone who needs oversized muscles to feel like somebody," Andi replied coolly.

Bull Neck flushed and jutted out his jaw. She could see he wanted to lay into her but Detective Lee silenced him with another look. She found herself pitying Detective Lee. Having to work with a misogynist shithead like Bull Neck had to be wearing.

"What can you tell us about this man?" the detective asked. 'Can you describe him better?"

Andi gave Lee the best description she could. "I think you should talk to Maggie Hoffman. She and Ashley and two of the others were still drinking when I left. Lauren walked with me back to my condo. She said she was headed home from my place but she might have gone back to Sloppy's instead. I don't know. I haven't talked to any of the others today. Can I leave now?"

Detective Lee took down her address and phone number in case they wanted to speak with her again and also gave her his card. She thanked him and walked outside. The sun was still shining but the day no longer felt so bright.

Her headache had returned, a dull pain low in the back of her skull. She felt heartsick and disoriented and no longer wanted to be alone. She didn't want to return to the office either–not as long as the two detectives were there.

She stood for several minutes listening to the traffic and finally walked in the direction of her parents' house, but before she reached it she found herself turning into Pandora and Zee's driveway.

She knocked on the door and waited. Sam answered holding Pandora's two year old daughter, Ariel.

"Can I come in?"

Samantha must have seen something in her face because she reached for Andi's hand and pulled her into the hallway.

# CHAPTER 14

S AM CLOSED the door behind Andi. Ariel leaned comfortably on Sam's shoulder with her thumb in her mouth, her eyes sleepy. Her lips curved in a smile around her thumb when she saw Andi.

Ariel's smile touched something deep inside Andi. Would she ever be blessed with children? For the first time in her life she found herself thinking beyond the near future. And realized she wanted a family of her own.

Sam touched her arm briefly. "Just let me put Ariel down for her nap and I'll make us some tea. Go on through to the kitchen and wait for me." She headed up a wide staircase with the toddler.

Andi followed the long hall back to the kitchen. Although she'd only been in the house once before it felt welcoming and comfortable. She was glad she hadn't gone to her mother's. Cass would have brushed off Ashley's murder and pushed her to have dinner with Angus Ames.

Once in the kitchen she wasn't sure what to do with herself so she stood at the windows to wait for Sam. The day-glo frisbees still marked the bases where she'd played whiffle ball with the kids and adults. She'd had a great deal of fun that day.

The whiffle ball game seemed a lifetime ago now. So much had happened to her since Saturday. A half sob escaped her lips and she put her fingers to her mouth. She needed to get a hold of herself. It wouldn't do to cry all over Sam, a woman she'd met only once before.

Taking a deep breath to calm her nerves, Andi turned away from the window and plopped down on one of the leather chairs in front of the cold fireplace. Her hands were shaking and she felt cold inside despite the warm day. She wrapped her arms around her middle, tucking her hands under her arms in an effort to warm them and keep them from shaking.

When Sam returned to the kitchen she wordlessly went about the task of making a pot of tea. She set some fresh-baked peanut butter cookies and two mugs on the tea tray and carried it over to where Andi sat. Taking the chair next to Andi, Sam handed Andi a steaming mug and then sipped at her own, still saying nothing.

The tea helped warm Andi on the inside. She drank down half the mug before she felt she could talk.

"Thank you. I needed this."

Sam smiled at her. "I've done nothing but make a friend a cup of tea and you're welcome."

Friend. Even though Andi barely knew Sam's or Pandora's family she had felt that she was in the home of friends. The knowledge loosened some of the tension she was holding in her body but she still didn't feel quite ready to speak about Ashley.

As if she understood, Sam began to talk. "You're probably wondering how I got hooked up with Pandora and Zee," she said, her tone light. She offered the cookies to Andi who refused and she set the tray down again.

"Nearly seven years ago now my husband walked out on me and the children when Sarah was only a baby. She was sickly and always crying because she didn't feel well." She shrugged one slim shoulder and frowned, her expression looking inward.

"I guess he couldn't take it." She looked at Andi. "I was devastated. And frightened. I had four young children depending on me and a job that barely covered our rent. After my husband left my oldest boy Luke tried to become the man of the house–even though he was only ten. He hooked up with a gang that used young kids to sneak into houses and steal. He did it to bring in money so he could help me buy food."

Andi could hear the pride in Sam's voice and wondered what it must have been like for a young mother to suddenly find herself shouldering the care of four young children by herself.

"Your stress levels must have been through the roof."

"You have no idea. Fortunately Pandora caught Luke one night sneaking into Zee's place. She tracked him down and offered him an honest way to earn money helping her out around this place."

Andi felt the tension in her body loosening as she listened to Sam's story. She understood that Sam was giving her time to pull herself together and marveled at the other woman's insight. Her mother would have either ignored Andi's feelings or brushed them aside as unimportant.

Sam smiled at her memories of that time. "It's a long story but the short version is that Zee saved Luke's and Pandora's lives when the gang leader came after them. They married and then they offered me the job of looking after them and the house. They insisted my family take over the third floor so I'd be available whenever they need me. I owe them everything. They gave me a safe and beautiful home for my children and steady employment doing what I love."

"I think they are fortunate to have you," Andi told her.

Sam smiled. "It's a two way street."

They sat in silence for several minutes, sipping tea and thinking their own thoughts.

"The body of someone I know was found this morning in the river," Andi blurted out.

"Oh dear. How awful for you. We hadn't heard."

"Her body was only found this morning so it might not have hit the news yet. The thing is, I was one of the last people to see her alive. I went out with some co-workers after work yesterday and she was one of them."

Andi told Sam about Sloppy's Happy Hour and the two detectives who had questioned her that morning.

"The senior detective, Detective Lee, didn't come out and say they suspected foul play but he also didn't say that Ashley's death was an accident. I don't know what to think. It's possible she decided to go for a swim after leaving Sloppy's and drowned. I know I was pretty drunk when I left. But she didn't *seem* drunk."

"I'm so very sorry for your loss," Sam said. "I know that doesn't help, but I'm sorry to hear that a vibrant young woman has died before her time. I can't believe that she was murdered. La Crosse has its problems like any other city but murder has never been high on that list."

Andi nodded and set down her empty tea cup. "I don't why I'm so upset about it. I didn't really know Ashley at all. I didn't even know her last name until the detective told me. But she seemed nice and she was harmless. I liked her. She drank and laughed and was flirting with a guy at the bar and enjoying herself. She didn't deserve to go out for Happy Hour and end up dead."

Andi felt pressure building in her chest and took a deep breath. "I was going to visit my mother–who probably isn't even home–but I found myself at your door instead. I'm not sure why." She looked at the empty tray. "Thank you for the cookies. I didn't even realize I ate them."

Sam smiled. It struck Andi that Sam's smile lent a sweet type of beauty to an otherwise ordinary face.

"I find cookies to be remarkably soothing, especially with a proper cup of tea," Sam told her. "I have to bake nearly every day to keep seven children and several adults in desserts."

Andi grabbed onto the subject change. "Does Perseus live here with you?"

"No, but Zee insists that he stay with us whenever he's in town. The house is certainly large enough and the children all adore him."

"Where–" The back door opened before Andi could find out where Perseus's home was. She heard voices and laughter. A moment later Pandora entered the kitchen followed by Zee and Perseus.

As large as the kitchen was, Andi felt it shrink with the presence of the two brothers. They were large, forceful men who seemed to command any space they occupied.

Perseus felt a pleasant smugness come over him when he saw Andi sitting in the kitchen. She had come to see him because she missed him. Good. It was only fair since she had been on his mind constantly since he'd left her condo on Monday. It was almost embarrassing how often he had thought about her.

In the next breath he realized that it was midday

Thursday and Andi should be in her office. He was across the kitchen and by her side in a second.

"What happened?" he demanded, looking down at her. "Is it Ames? What has he done?"

Andi found both her hands wrapped in Percy's large warm ones. His concern and his warmth brought tears to her eyes. She clenched her jaw and blinked back the tears that seemed to flow all too easily but Perseus noticed them anyway.

Before she could say anything Perseus pulled Andi to her feet and moved her to the couch. He sat beside her and placed his arm around her shoulders, gently easing her against his side.

Zee raised his eyebrow at him but Perseus ignored the gesture. He didn't care what his brother thought. Something was wrong or Andi wouldn't be there in the middle of a work day. Despite his worry, the fact that she'd come to him for help warmed him down to his toes.

Pandora and Zee joined them in front of the fireplace. Sam made more tea and piled more cookies on the tray and soon they were all sitting with Andi, waiting to hear what she had to say. After she repeated the news about Ashley's death no one spoke for several minutes.

"Ashley isn't the first young woman who's gone out drinking with friends and ended up pulled from the river," Pandora told them.

"It's a river town and a college town. It's bound to happen. How many others have there been?" Zee reached over and clasped his wife's hand. "I can't believe I haven't heard about this before."

Pandora smiled at her husband. "You don't know everything, you know."

Zee harrumphed and demanded his wife fill them in.

"Another woman was pulled from the river two years ago. It only made the news for a couple days."

"But there have been more?" Perseus asked.

"I don't think anyone has really noticed the pattern, to be honest," Pandora told him. "I only know because I pay attention to that sort of thing."

"What sort of thing?" Perseus asked. "What are you two talking about?"

"Three women have been pulled from the river over the last five years, counting Ashley. All were attractive young women who went drinking with friends in the historic district and were never seen alive again. No marks were found on their bodies so the police concluded they went down to the river for some reason, fell in, and drowned because they were too drunk to swim or pull themselves out."

"I can't believe Ashley was so drunk that she fell into the river and drowned." Andi shook her head. "Those women go to Sloppy's Happy Hour nearly every week. I was the only one who showed any sign of having too much to drink and that's because I always limit myself to one glass of wine and last night I drank four mojitos."

"Mmmm, I love a good mojito." Pandora licked her lips. "But I could never drink four. I don't like being out of control so I rarely drink to excess."

Zee snorted. "You *never* drink to excess and the only time I've seen you out of control is when we–"

"Zee!" Zee grinned at his wife, obviously pleased he'd made her blush.

Andi watched the byplay between Pandora and Zee and felt envious. What would it feel like to know that someone loved you above all others?

She felt Perseus's knuckles gently rubbing up and down

her arm and wondered if he realized he was doing it. She had been trying to sit as straight as possible despite his arm around her shoulders but the urge to curl against him was becoming difficult to ignore. She straightened her spine further.

"So . . . if Ashley didn't fall into the river and was too drunk to pull herself out, what do you think happened to her?" Sam asked Pandora. She handed out more cookies before settling back into her chair.

"I think La Crosse has a serial killer who either isn't a local or can go a long time between kills. If he's not a local he only kills when he comes to town and the circumstances are right," Pandora answered. "Obviously it needs to be warm enough for people to believe the women actually went swimming."

Andi's stomach clenched. "A serial killer? Here?" she whispered.

"You're thinking either a businessman or a college student." Zee looked at his wife, who nodded at him.

"Exactly. It would be interesting to do a little research and see if there have been other young women who had gone drinking with friends and were later pulled from rivers anywhere else in the state, or even in the country."

"I can check on that," Zee told her. "Has there been any speculation about a serial killer in the papers?"

Pandora shook her head. "No. The kills are too far between. And college students are notorious for drinking too much and pulling foolish pranks. I wasn't confident enough to take my suspicions to the police. They have a lot more information than I do and I knew they'd simply blow me off."

Zee looked at Andi. "We'll try to find out what the police know about what happened to your friend. I suggest that you skip Sloppy's Happy Hours until we get to the bottom of whatever's going on."

"You think the killer is somehow connected to Sloppy's?" Andi thought about the body builder leaning over Ashley when she was leaving with Lauren. Had Ashley left the bar with a serial killer? She shuddered.

"I enjoyed myself last night but I'm paying for it today," she told Zee with a rueful smile. "Believe me, staying away from Sloppy's won't be a hardship." She made a mental note to warn Maggie about the bar when she saw her at work the next day.

# CHAPTER 15

ALTHOUGH ANDI HADN'T PLANNED to stay long, the others seemed relaxed and happy to sit in the kitchen and talk so she stayed until the time came for Pandora and Zee to fetch the children from summer day camp.

Sliding out from under Perseus's warm and comfortable arm she stood as well. "I need to get going too," she told them, smoothing down her wrinkled skirt. "I've taken up enough of your time."

She turned to Sam. "Sam, thank you. Thank you for the delicious cookies and tea and thank you for giving me some of your time."

Sam surprised Andi by reaching out and giving her a big hug. "You're welcome here anytime, Andi. Consider us all your friends."

"That's right," Pandora called out as she headed out the back door. "You're one of us now."

Andi hadn't experienced many hugs in her life and she found herself stiffening in Sam's arms but the woman continued to hold on until Andi finally hugged her back.

"There, that wasn't so hard, was it?" Sam said with a smile as she released Andi and gave her a little pat on the arm. "You'll find that we're a touchy-feely family. Lots of hugs in this household. I'll warn you now that there will be more if you continue to visit."

Andi found herself smiling. "Is that a threat?"

"More like a promise." Sam gathered up the tray of empty mugs with Perseus's help. The baby monitor on the old buffet squawked.

"There's Ariel. Right on time. I swear that little girl has an uncannily accurate inner time clock. That's the end of the peace until the younger kids go to bed. Come back soon, Andi. Tomorrow if you want. You don't need a special invite. Come for dinner. I always cook enough to feed extra mouths."

Sam left the kitchen and Andi realized with a jolt that she was alone with Perseus. Now would be the time to apologize for kicking him out of her condo Monday night but she didn't know how to bring it up. She was searching for the right words when Perseus surprised her by tucking a piece of hair that had escaped her bun behind her ear.

"Are you going to be all right?" he asked.

"Of course." The gentleness of his touch made her throat tighten. "Why wouldn't I be?"

Perseus wrapped his arms loosely around her and looked into her eyes. She could clearly see the gold flecking his green irises. His lashes were thick and lush, chestnut like his hair. He had beautiful eyes.

"You've had a rough week and someone you knew just died unexpectedly. No one would be all right after that. Where are you headed now? Back to the office?"

Andi shook her head. "No. I'm going to walk home, feed

Spook, and take a long hot soak." She smiled ruefully. "I was a bit hung over this morning after all those mojitos," she admitted. "More than a bit, to be honest. I'm a lightweight when it comes to alcohol."

"That's nothing to be ashamed of." Perseus took her hand and pulled her toward the back door. "Come on. I'll drive you home."

Andi stiffened. She didn't want him feeling sorry for her. "You don't have to do that. I mean, thank you, but it's not that far. I can walk."

Perseus stopped and looked at her, obviously irritated. "I'm not offering because I feel I *have* to, Andromeda. I'm offering because I *want* to."

"I . . ." Why not? If she was honest with herself she really didn't have the energy to walk home. What harm could letting Perseus take her home do? "In that case, yes, thank you. I could use a lift."

"Good. It's not a big deal."

But it *was* a big deal to her. Perseus made her feel off balance. She was attracted to him and didn't know what to do with that, especially after he'd rejected her. When he was near she felt quivery and a little breathless. Every cell in her body seemed to be tuned in to him and she didn't know what to do about it. This was uncharted territory for her.

They were at her condo in less than ten minutes. Perseus took her hand and held it tight before Andi could make her escape from the car. "Come out with me later."

"Oh, no. Thank you but I can't." She tugged her hand free and stepped out of the car, leaning down to thank him through the open window.

"Feed your Spook, take a hot soak and a nap," he told her.

She couldn't see his eyes behind his dark glasses but she knew they were focused on her. "I intend to."

"Good. Wear jeans and boots. I'll pick you up at six." He rolled up the window and drove off before Andi could tell him she didn't want to see him later.

Which was a lie anyway, if she was going to be honest with herself.

The thought of seeing Perseus in a few hours drove off all feelings of fatigue. She ran up the three flights of stairs to her condo and wondered where he planned to take her. Nowhere fancy since he'd told her to wear jeans.

She fed the kitten, took a long soak and a nap, and was standing on the sidewalk in front of her condo at six sharp. She heard the engine from two blocks away before she saw the large Harley turn down her street.

Andi stepped inside the foyer to her building until the bike passed but it pulled to the curb in front of her building. Who did he know inside? She didn't think any of her neighbors associated with bikers.

As unfamiliar as she was with motorcycles she knew the one out front was a thing of beauty. Big, sleek, and powerful, it was shiny black with chrome trim that flashed in the sun and burgundy and gold lightning bolts painted on the gas tank. The essence of testosterone, the bike managed to look beautiful and at the same time dangerous.

Andi's stomach fluttered at the sight.

The bike's rider looked like a biker ninja, dressed in form-fitting black leather pants and jacket with a black helmet that had a dark tinted face shield. The burgundy lightning bolts repeated across the jacket's biceps.

More testosterone than she'd ever seen in one package. Wow. Her knees weakened.

The rider pulled off his helmet and grinned at her through the glass door. Double wow. Andi's eyes widened with shock. She could feel the pulse in her neck beat faster.

Perseus crooked a finger at her and pointed to the seat behind him.

She had never ridden on a motorcycle. Didn't know anyone who owned a motorcycle. Everything she knew about them was tied up with her parents' disdain of those who rode them as somehow being "less". Less intelligent. Lower on the social scale. To be ignored and avoided.

She stared at Perseus for several long moments before gathering her courage and walking outside.

Perseus shut off the bike's engine and set the kickstand, swinging a leg off the bike to stand beside it.

Oh sweet Jesus, she thought, trying to catch her breath. No one in their right mind could think this man was less in any way. Perseus looked hot and powerful. Black leather hugged his muscled thighs and broad chest. He was a man among men. No–he was a *god* among men. Heat began to gather low in her belly. She wanted this man in the worst way.

"Ever been on one before?"

She could see the laughter in his eyes, as if he knew exactly what she'd been thinking. She shook her head and uttered a weak "no".

"Well you're in for a treat." Perseus unhooked the spare helmet which was also decorated with a red lightening bolt and a bundle that turned out to be another leather jacket.

"Pan let me borrow her gear. Put these on. You can be my biker chick." He gave her a slow, wicked smile that showed the dimple in his left cheek and made her want to melt in his arms.

The jacket felt as soft and supple as warm butter. It had a shiny asymmetrical zipper and a notched collar decorated with stainless studs. It fit like a glove. Andi loved it. She rubbed her hands up her arms and hugged herself. The jacket made her feel sexy and wicked. Daring.

Perseus gave her a blatantly thorough up and down. The heat in his eyes when he finished told her he approved of what he saw.

"The helmets are linked so we can talk," he told her. "Hop on and hold tight."

"Where are we going?"

"We're going to take the river road south on the Minnesota side, crossover and find someplace to eat, then come back on the river road on the Wisconsin side. You game?"

Other than drinking at Sloppy's–which had turned out badly in more ways than one–it had been a long while since Andi had tried something new. She felt excitement fizz in her blood as she nodded. She put on the helmet and climbed on the bike behind Perseus.

She tried to sit straight and grab the sides of his jacket but Perseus took one of her hands and pulled it forward so it wrapped right around him.

"Think of us as one unit," he told her through the helmet mic.

She had to spread her knees around his thighs to scoot close enough to wrap both her arms around his waist. The position felt incredibly intimate. Her entire torso pressed against his strong back. But when he started the bike and she felt the power throbbing beneath her and between her legs she thought she'd never felt anything so sexy.

She groaned and Perseus chuckled in her ear. "Wait 'til we get going," he said, his voice low and intimate in her ear.

He swung the bike in an arc and headed back up the street. They crossed the blue bridge high over the river to

Minnesota and ten minutes later were cruising down the river road, hemmed in by steep bluffs on their right and the wide expanse of the Mississippi on the left.

Perseus handled the large bike with ease and Andi soon relaxed. It didn't take long for her to realize that the ride was all about becoming one with not only the bike and Perseus, but the terrain as well. She held tight to him and leaned into the curves, exhilarated by the sense of freedom the bike gave.

When Perseus pulled into an overlook to watch a flock of pelicans on the river it was the most natural thing in the world to turn into his arms and kiss him. Afterward they stood together with their arms around each other's waists and watched the large black and white birds with their strange beaks skim barely above the water's surface in a graceful glide until it was time to find someplace for dinner.

They ended up in a popular local hamburger joint that advertised handmade beef patties and steak fries. People of all ages including the very young and the very old ate off paper plates side by side at long picnic-style tables. Conversation and laughter filled the joint.

Andi ate her simple meal of burger and fries with enthusiasm. It didn't take much cajoling to talk Perseus into ice cream after. They wandered across the street to an old-fashioned ice cream parlor and ordered a couple double scoop cones.

They sat shoulder to shoulder on a bench, eating their ice cream while they kept an eye on the bike and people watched. The business district along the river was busy with families and couples and groups of teens enjoying the beautiful early summer evening. Pontoon party boats and powerboats plied the river to their left. Music poured from a busy bar down the street.

Andi sighed with contentment. "I don't think I've ever enjoyed myself this much on a date before," she said, turning to look at the handsome man beside her. "Thank you. You've completely blown my ignorant views on bikers."

"Good to hear, although there is a certain class of bikers you might want to steer clear of. Like any group of people there are good and not so good members." He shifted his cone to his left hand and clasped Andi's free hand in his right, intertwining their fingers. "I'm glad you're having fun. I enjoy your company, Andromeda."

He inspected her face and felt satisfied with what he saw. She looked genuinely happy for the first time since they'd met. Her blue eyes sparkled and her cheeks had color. She'd worn her thick blond hair in two braids that made her look carefree. He liked the look.

The sun was setting as they drove back into La Crosse, streaking the sky and river's surface with bands of rose and gold. The blue bridges rose on their left. They'd come full circle. Andi hated to see the evening end. The hours with Perseus had felt magical and had allowed her to leave behind everything that was dragging on her.

Reality came slamming back along with the traffic lights and noise of a summer evening in a college town.

Perseus pulled to the curb in front of her condo and Andi hopped off the bike. Removing the helmet and Pandora's jacket completed the transformation back into Andromeda White.

"I don't want to leave Zee's bike unattended or I'd walk you to your door." Perseus dismounted the bike and took off his helmet. "But I can at least see you safely inside the building."

Andi unlocked the foyer door and turned to say goodnight but Perseus pushed her gently inside. He wrapped her in his arms and bent his head so their lips were only inches apart, a question in his eyes.

Andi didn't hesitate. She leaned into him, closing the distance. She kissed Perseus with everything she had, pressing against him and running her hands up to cradle his face. It was the first time she'd ever initiated a kiss. When they broke apart they were both breathing hard. Perseus choked out a half laugh and leaned his forehead against hers.

"I want to see you again, Andi. I have to leave town for a few days to take care of some business but I'd like to call you when I return."

"I don't even know what you do for work. We never talked about it."

Perseus reluctantly dropped his arms and stepped back. "Nothing glamorous, I assure you. In fact most people would label my job downright dull. I'm a turnaround specialist. I help failing companies get back on their feet. I'm at a critical stage with a company in Chicago at the moment. Sometimes I have to do a fair amount of hand holding and this is one of them or I wouldn't leave. Since meeting you La Crosse has become a much more interesting place."

She should have known that Percy's work involved helping others in some way. He had all the makings of a white knight. "I think it sounds interesting and challenging."

Not wanting him to see how disappointed she was that he couldn't extend their evening she turned to unlock the stairwell door, but before she got it open Perseus grabbed her shoulder and turned her back.

"You never answered my question. Can I see you again when I get back?"

"I'd like that."

Perseus smiled. "Great. I'll call you while I'm out of town. I need to know you're okay." He kissed her briefly and left. Andi stood in the foyer with her keys in her hand and listened until she could no longer hear the big bike's engine before heading upstairs.

# CHAPTER 16

As soon as Andi came through the door the kitten greeted her with indignant mews and chased her into the kitchen area demanding more food. She fed Spook and then sat on the floor to cuddle and play with him until he curled up for a nap. All the while her brain relived every moment of her date with Perseus.

She had never met a man who attracted her the way he did. He was not only interesting and incredibly attractive, he also made her feel tingly and alive in a way she'd never experienced before. When she was with him he made her feel like a different person. He made her feel that she had value apart from Cepheus and Cass White and Cepheus White Sports.

Best of all Perseus had no reason to curry favor with her because of her father's company. He spent time with her because he wanted to.

Andi turned off the lights, picked up Spook, and moved to the couch. She could already feel that the tiny kitten had put on weight even though she'd had him less than a week. His golden yellow eyes blinked at her and she kissed the top of his head before settling him on her chest.

The river was always busy on beautiful summer evenings and tonight was no exception. She watched the red and green lights of motorboats and party pontoon boats as they maneuvered out of the way of a flotilla of empty barges headed upriver. She and Perseus had ridden by that same flotilla on their way back to La Crosse after their dinner and ice cream.

Andi had talked with Perseus about her parents. As far back as she could remember they had controlled her life. She had never experienced the "fly the nest" syndrome that most teens went through. They had placed her in private boarding schools from first grade on. She'd attended college year round and graduated in three years. Somehow there was never any time to meet boys and date.

After graduation she'd applied for jobs outside her father's company because she wanted to find her own way in the world. She'd been turned down until she realized no one would hire her against her father's wishes. She'd given up her dreams and gone to work for her father's company.

She believed her parents meant well, that they were grooming her to take over Cepheus White Sports when her father was ready to retire, and she had tried her hardest to fill their expectations because she felt she owed them.

Talking with Perseus helped her see that she no longer felt that way. It had even helped her see that she had *never* felt that way, not really. She'd simply given up the battle.

She knew that following in her father's footsteps wasn't what she wanted. She would never be happy running CWS. She didn't enjoy the deal making or socializing with people she didn't care about or even like. Odds were she'd run the company into the ground. She simply wasn't a good fit.

The realization both frightened and excited her. If following in her father's footsteps wasn't her path, what was?

She needed to give it some serious thought before she told her parents she was leaving Cepheus White Sports. They were not going to be pleased.

"Big changes coming, Spook," she told the kitten. "We need to make plans." She set Spook on the arm of the couch while she grabbed a pad of paper and her favorite fountain pen, a vintage 1930s jade green Schaeffer that her mother had given her upon graduation.

The green of the pen reminded her of Perseus's eyes. She hoped he called her while he was away. She already wanted to see him again in the worst way.

When he called she was going to invite him for dinner, she decided. Maybe in the privacy of her condo she could convince him to do more than kiss her. She was bursting with curiosity to see where his kisses could lead.

She forced her thoughts back to the task at hand, listing her strengths and the things she enjoyed doing and jobs that were related to them. The list was short, but it was a start.

She dreamt of Perseus and woke up to the realization that it was Friday and she still hadn't resolved the issue of Angus Ames. Then she remembered the resolution she'd made the previous night to break away from her father's company. Refusing dinner with Angus would be a start.

In honor of her new outlook, Andi took the elevator to the seventh floor, riding with several women she didn't know who were discussing their plans for the weekend–the kind of normal activities that friends and families engaged in. Activities like playing ball and having a picnic. Just what she'd done with Pandora's family. The memory brought a smile to her face and lifted her spirits.

The sight of Maggie in her cubicle reminded Andi of Ashley's death and wiped the smile from her face. Maggie was tied up talking with a customer so Andi headed straight to her office.

She hadn't seen any of the women she'd gone to Sloppy's with since she had learned about Ashley's death but she felt sure that Detective Lee and Bull Neck must have interviewed them by now. Andi knew she should offer her condolences. The others had all known Ashley well and had to be shaken up by what had happened to their friend.

A friend would say something to them. She wanted to be their friend.

She dropped her tote beside her desk and headed back toward Maggie's cubicle.

As soon as Maggie finished the call she was on she whipped off her headset. "You heard about Ash?" she asked. Shadows bruised the skin under Maggie's eyes. Her red curls had been pulled back into a ponytail and her freckles stood out in her pale, drawn face.

"Yes, I heard. I'm so sorry, Maggie. Did the detectives talk to you?"

Maggie nodded. "I don't get it. I've known Ash forever and I've never known her to do something so stupid. Whatever possessed her to walk down to the river?"

"Could Ashley have walked down to the river and then decided to go for a swim?" Andi asked carefully. She didn't think it would be smart to mention Pandora's theory. Pandora had no proof that there was a serial killer targeting young women in the area and Andi didn't want to start a panic if it wasn't true.

"That's what the detective said." Maggie looked angry and hurt. "Why didn't she ask one of us to go with her? We would have talked her out of going for a swim."

"Did you leave Sloppy's together? Lauren walked me

home–for which I was very grateful–and said she was headed home herself to study."

Maggie shook her head. "I left with Laura and Cathy. Ash was talking to Steve and didn't want to leave so we left her."

Andi caught her breath. "Steve? Was he the guy who looked like a body builder?"

"Yeah. He and Ash have been dancing around each other for months now. They used to date but she broke it off. He still asks her out and she says no because she doesn't want to get tied down but it's stupid because we all know he's the only one she has eyes for. Had eyes for. Shit."

Tears welled up in Maggie's eyes. She grabbed her large purse and pulled out a packet of tissues. "Shit," she said again. "Sorry."

Andi patted her awkwardly on the shoulder. "I'm so sorry for your loss. I only met Ashley the one time but I liked her." She waited for Maggie to get herself under control again. "Do you think . . ."

She stopped. There was no tactful way to phrase what she wanted to know. She tried again. "You don't think Steve could have hurt Ashley, do you?"

Maggie's eyes widened. "Steve? You think he drowned Ash? No. Impossible. Steve's not the brightest of men but he has a good heart and he honestly cares–cared–about Ash."

Two lights began to blink on Maggie's console. She picked up her headset. "I have to get back to work before the super comes looking to see why I'm slacking off."

Andi hesitated. "Could you let me know when Ashley's family holds the service for her? I'd like to pay my respects."

Maggie nodded without speaking and Andi headed back to her office, thinking. If Ashley had been dating Steve and broke it off it was possible that Steve was more upset about it than Maggie realized. What if he and Ashley had left Sloppy's together, maybe walked down to the river to talk, and had an argument? Maybe there was some angry shoving involved and Ashley fell in.

She shook her head. The scenario didn't feel right. Someone would have seen the pair leave the bar together. The truth was, she didn't want there to be a serial killer in La Crosse. The thought of an unknown killer targeting young women was too frightening. She wanted Ashley's death to be either an accident or a one-time lover's spat gone wrong.

Andi made herself get back to work on the spreadsheet she'd left the day before but her heart wasn't in it. She had never enjoyed sitting at a desk all day but today she felt more antsy than usual. She chalked her restlessness up to the decision she'd made last night to leave her job. While she knew she had to go about it in stages she was anxious to get on with whatever came next.

She had to keep pulling her attention back to the numbers on her computer screen. Thoughts of Ashley's death or her date the previous night with Perseus kept distracting her. Somehow she managed to make progress on the spreadsheet until her father's admin assistant interrupted.

"Mr. White would like to see you in his office, Miss White." Spencer hung up before Andi could think of an excuse not to see her father.

She hung up the phone and jabbed her fingers into her hair in frustration. She knew her father wanted to make sure she was having dinner with Angus Ames even though she hadn't agreed to do so.

How she longed just to walk away from her office and the date and never have to think about them again.

*Independence happens one step at a time. Start with Angus Ames.*

The phone buzzed again. This time it was Gus from the lobby. "A dress bag has arrived for you from Darling's Boutique. Would you like me to bring it up to your office, Miss Andromeda?"

Darling's Boutique was her mother's go-to shop for one of a kind designer clothing. Her parents were ganging up on her from both sides. She had to bite her tongue to keep from telling Gus to throw the dress in the trash. He wouldn't understand. Besides, he was only doing his job. Cass often sent dresses for Andi to the office and Gus usually handled them. It wouldn't be right to take her frustration out on him.

"Thank you, Gus, but I'll pick it up on my way out."

There was no point in putting off the confrontation with her father. She might as well tell him that she had no intention of having dinner with Angus Ames that night or any other night.

Maybe he'd fire her. The thought brightened her mood.

# CHAPTER 17

ANDI CLIMBED the twenty-six steps to the eighth floor and let herself through the fire escape door. Her father's admin scowled at her. She knew he didn't approve of her using the stairs. In Spencer's world ladylike women always took the elevator, therefore Andi was not a lady and deserved a scowl.

"Hello, Spencer. Would you tell my father I'm here, please?" Andi didn't give the admin time to call her father. She strode straight for her father's closed office door with Spencer scurrying behind her.

"Miss White! You *must* let me announce you."

"I'll announce myself." She pulled open the doors and stepped into her father's office.

"You wanted to see me?"

Spencer fretted in the doorway, obviously wanting to let his boss know that he wasn't at fault for her rude behavior. Andi turned and pulled the doors closed in Spencer's face. The action gave her courage. She had never cared for Spencer's prissy attitude.

She turned to face her father.

"If you called me up here to remind me that I have a date

tonight with Angus Ames you can forget it. I told you I don't want to have dinner with him. Take my condo. I'd rather rent a small apartment somewhere than be forced to date a man I don't like."

She didn't take a close look at her father until she stopped speaking. He sat behind his massive desk drumming the fingers of one hand on a file folder. His mouth was set in a grim line, his eyes hard.

Were her mortgage papers in that manila folder? She focused on it and her father's hand and had a sudden, exciting thought–if her father offered to pay off the mort-gage on her condo in exchange for a dinner date with Ames she could definitely put up with the pompous man for one meal. She started to speak but her father interrupted.

"Your mother picked up a dress for you to wear on your date tonight with Angus. It should be here shortly. Be sure to leave early so you have time to get ready. Angus prides himself on being punctual and he'll expect it of you as well. I've given him your address and he'll pick you up at six thirty."

The news that her father had given Angus her address angered her, but even more troubling was the fact that he hadn't heard a word she'd spoken about not having dinner with Angus. Were her parents so used to her doing whatever they asked that they no longer listened to her?

She should never have gone to work for her father. She could see that so clearly now. *Don't look back. You can only move forward. Remember independence.*

"You shouldn't have given out my address. And I can dress myself, Dad. I don't need Mother's help."

"Tonight is important, Andromeda. You have to make a good impression and your mother has impeccable taste. You'll wear whatever she's chosen."

"I'm not having dinner with Angus Ames. I've told him no, I've told you no, and I've told Mother no. What do I have to do to get you to understand that I mean no?"

She stepped forward. It wasn't until she stood next to the desk that she realized her father had gone pale beneath his golf tan. Two worry lines formed a crease between his brow. She saw his hand tremble before he snatched it from the folder and placed it in his lap.

Her anger immediately forgotten, Andi rounded the desk and squatted beside her father.

For the first time in her memory her father looked his age. A tall handsome man with a head full of thick dark hair and deep blue eyes that resembled her own, Cepheus White had always been the picture of health. She knew that he stuck to a religious regimen of golf, tennis, and swimming that kept him fit and trim. She had never seen the slightest sign of weakness in him until that moment and it frightened her.

"Dad? What is it? Are you okay? Should I call a doctor?"

He shook his head and sighed. "I don't need a doctor."

"You don't look well. Please let me call Dr. Davy for you." Dr. Davy was her father's friend and a GP.

"I'm sorry, Andi. I've made a terrible mistake." Her father sighed heavily.

The defeated tone in her father's voice scared Andi even more than the fear that something was amiss with his health. She sat back on her heels and studied him.

"I don't understand. What are you sorry about? What mistake?"

She stood and moved back as Cepheus pushed to his feet.

"Let's sit by the windows." He took one of the deeply cushioned leather chairs and waited for Andi to join him.

Andi didn't want to sit. She stood behind the chair across

from her father and gripped the back while she waited for him to speak. Something was wrong and she had a feeling she wasn't going to like whatever it was he had to say.

Cepheus nodded once when he realized she had no intention of sitting. "Fair enough. You know that Angus Ames is our largest supplier of the clothing we buy to silkscreen and monogram and then sell wholesale and retail?"

Andi nodded. "Yes. You were excited when you signed the contract with his company."

"Right. What you might not know is that over the last two years Angus's company has become our *only* supplier of clothing. He gives us excellent terms and has always delivered on time. He doesn't require us to carry large inventories which lets us keep more free capital on hand. He also never squawks or penalizes us if we add to an order or decrease one. In other words, he works with us. It's been a beneficial partnership for both of us."

Andi stared at her father while a greasy ball of dread began to form in her belly. "*Until now*. It's been beneficial until now. That's what you're trying to say isn't it."

Cepheus closed his eyes briefly and nodded. "Yes. It's been beneficial until now. Please believe me when I tell you I had no idea that Angus wanted you."

Andi released the chair back with one hand and pressed it to her belly. "Define 'want', Dad. Just what does Angus want with me?"

The comment she'd made to Perseus about Angus wanting to nail Cepheus White's virgin daughter flashed into her mind. She held her gaze steady on her father but he wouldn't meet her eyes.

"Dad? What's going on?"

"Your mother invited Angus to the June gala specifically to see you–at his request."

"That explains the dress that was barely there and lending me her diamonds."

Her father had the decency to blush at least. He cleared his throat. "Yes, well, you were supposed to accept Angus's invitation to dinner that night."

"But I didn't because Perseus told Angus I was dining with him whatever night it was."

"Yes."

Andi could see it all now. "So Mother came up with the bright idea of ambushing me at your house by inviting me for dinner without telling me that Angus would be there."

Her father nodded.

Disgusted, Andi glared at him. "Why can't you and Mother accept that I do not want to have *anything* to do with Angus Ames? I'm your daughter for crying out loud. Your only child. You should be protecting me, not siding with some disgusting old lecher."

"Angus has threatened to withhold all future shipments until you agree to have dinner with him."

"*What?*" Andi couldn't believe her ears.

"I said–"

"Never mind, I heard you. I can't believe what I heard but I heard you."

She stepped around to the front of the chair and dropped into it. "How could you let yourself get backed into a corner like that, Dad?"

Shame warred with embarrassment in her father's eyes. "I didn't realize what kind of game Angus was playing," he admitted. "He offered the company good terms and I couldn't see any downside so I signed the contracts. I didn't know that his endgame was you, Andromeda. It never occurred to me."

"Did Mother know?"

Her father hesitated. "I don't know . . . I don't think so."

Suddenly Andi understood her mother's endgame. "Mother wants me to snag Angus Ames, doesn't she? She wants an alliance with your biggest supplier and marriage is the best way to accomplish that. She encouraged him. I might as well be living in England's regency era when marriages were arranged for power and profit."

Unable to look at her father anymore she sprang from the chair and went to stand in front of the large windows. Traffic filled the busy street below and pedestrians–many tourists exploring the city's historic district–bustled along the sidewalks with their shopping bags and ice cream cones. She wondered if any of their mothers were heartless manipulators like her own.

"So, how long would it take you to find a new supplier to replace Angus?" she asked without turning around.

"Too long. It takes time to vet factories and set up a pipeline. The raw materials have to be purchased and the goods manufactured. Six months at the soonest. You know this is a cutthroat business. Our competitors are breathing down our backs waiting for me to screw up so they can grab our biggest clients."

Andi thought about the laundry baskets filled with bundles of clothing waiting to be monogrammed that she'd seen on the third floor. "Surely we have enough inventory to carry us for six months. It will be a scramble but you can do it." She turned to look at her father.

He shook his head. "We went to a just-in-time delivery system with Angus earlier this year so we wouldn't have to tie up cash carrying inventory. We buy only enough to fill orders for immediate delivery. We don't have any stock on hand to tide us over while we look for an alternate supplier."

"So what you're telling me is that Cepheus White Sports is screwed unless I agree to have dinner with Angus Ames."

"Not just have dinner with him," mumbled her father.

A wave of cold anger washed through Andi. "You can't expect me to sleep with the man. That's going too far, even for Mother."

Cepheus sighed. "It's not just your mother who wants an alliance," he said quietly. "Angus wants to marry you. He's been looking for a suitable wife and has decided that you would be ideal, especially since you are the heir to the company."

For a long moment Andi couldn't take in the words. She moved to stand in front of her father's chair. "It's not just Mother playing matchmaker–you're as guilty as she is. You knew Angus wanted more than dinner. The three of you cooked up this scheme without any consideration as to how I'd feel about it. You put the company ahead of my happiness. Again."

She watched her father steadily. "But then you always have, haven't you?" she added softly. Even though she'd known somewhere deep inside that her parents cared more for Cepheus White Sports than they did for her it hurt to have the knowledge out in the open.

Her hands were shaking, she realized. She needed to get out of her father's office. She turned away and strode toward the door. "I'm leaving now. I won't be back. I'm through with Cepheus White Sports and I'm through with you and Mother."

Before she could reach the door her father's voice lashed out at her. "If you walk out of here now several hundred people will lose their jobs before month's end. Think about that, Andromeda. If the company goes under all those unemployed people will have only you to blame."

Andi pressed her forehead to the wooden door and closed her eyes. "No Dad, they'll have you and Mother to blame because you're the ones who set this up. I'm only a pawn in the despicable game you're playing."

An image of Maggie and Lauren and Ashley drinking and laughing at Sloppy's popped into her mind. Lauren needed the job to support herself until she got her own yoga studio going. Maggie helped support her younger brother who was excelling in college. Most everyone who worked for CWS had families to support. They relied on their jobs to pay the rent or mortgages and put food on their tables. Losing their jobs would be a hardship for them.

She couldn't put them all out of work. "Damn you."

She turned to face her father again. "I'll have dinner with Angus Ames tonight. I will also do my best to make him understand that I'll make his life a living hell if he insists on marrying me."

Her father stood, the relief plain on his face. "Thank you. I knew you'd do the right thing. I'll make it up to you somehow."

The look Andi shot him put a stop to anything more he'd intended to say. "You can never make this up to me," she said softly and walked out.

# CHAPTER 18

Andi stood in the lobby of her condo waiting for Angus Ames to pick her up. She didn't want the man in her home so had decided it would be better to be waiting downstairs when he arrived.

Checking the slim, diamond-banded watch on her wrist she saw that she still had ten minutes to go. In her nervousness she'd gotten ready far too early. She contemplated going back upstairs but didn't want to risk it if Angus arrived early. The whole point was to keep as much distance as possible between him and her life.

What a bloody mess. Anger warred with hurt inside her as she paced back and forth from door to mailboxes to stairwell to door again. Her father had put her in an untenable position. Sacrifice one for the good of the many.

Her life and happiness in exchange for job security for hundreds of CWS employees. Her only hope was to turn Angus against her.

A sleek black Audi pulled to the curb in front of the building and Angus Ames stepped out of the driver's side.

Andi took several deep breaths and pasted a stiff smile on her face before going out to greet him.

"Ah, Andromeda, right on time. I like that in a woman. You look incredibly lovely tonight." He came around the car and opened the passenger door for her.

For a brief moment Andi froze. Her feet refused to step toward the car and she felt the first tendrils of panic wind through her belly. She couldn't do this. No matter what the consequences were she couldn't date a man she didn't like.

It took her several more breaths to steady herself and regain control of her feet.

"Thank you, Mr. Ames." She slid into the soft leather seat and buckled her seatbelt. The car smelled of new leather and a faint spice she couldn't name. She watched as Angus walked around the front of car. He looked immaculate as always in a charcoal gray suit that looked custom fit to his slim body. His hair was perfectly coiffed.

He reminded her of the old Ken dolls, Barbie's supposed boyfriend.

Angus slid into the driver's seat. His arm brushed hers and she shifted closer to her door.

"You must call me Angus." It came out as more of a command than a request.

"After all, we'll be seeing quite a bit of each other, at least until the wedding." He turned his head to smile at her, his teeth too white in his tanned face, his dark eyes cold and assessing.

His certainty that there would be a wedding put Andi's back up. She managed to rein in her temper but it took a great deal of effort. She had a feeling the entire evening was going to be more of the same–Angus pissing her off so she had to fight for composure. What fun.

"Very well . . . Angus . . . I'm surprised you have to stoop to blackmail to get a date. I would think that plenty of pretty young women would be only too happy to go out with you." Unlike me, she added silently.

So much for playing it cool.

Angus chuckled. "So the beautiful kitten has some claws. Good, I like a fiesty woman although I prefer you limit it to when we're in bed. Let me warn you–it will not do for you to be rude to me in public, my dear. I won't put up with it. If you think you can subvert the deal I made with your parents by being unpleasant I can tell you now that it won't work. I will get what I want. I always do."

The man was insufferable. "You presume too much if you think I'll agree to go to bed with you."

She turned her head to look at him. Angus was watching her, his lips curled in a knowing smirk. The bastard didn't believe her. Was his ego so inflated that he honestly believed he could have any woman he wanted?

"I'm a little surprised," Andi continued, determined to wipe the smirk from Angus's face. "You can't possibly want to spend an evening with someone who not only doesn't like you but also doesn't want to be with you."

Angus raised his eyebrows. "What does liking have to do with anything? This is a business deal, Andromeda, not a love match," he chided. "I need a beautiful, young wife who knows how to behave at business functions and can play hostess when I entertain. I also need her to produce offspring to leave my empire to. Thanks to your mother's training you fit the bill. You also happen to be the most beautiful woman I've ever met. Therefore you are my choice."

He pulled the car away from the curb and turned north.

Andi was having difficulty believing her ears. Angus sounded as if choosing a wife based on the criteria he mentioned was the most natural thing in the world. He really was a throwback to medieval times.

He continued before she could tell him what she thought of his attitude.

"I have a lot to offer a wife. You can be assured that you will have the finest of everything," he continued, ignoring Andi's seething anger. "I own five houses—all large show places, all fully staffed. You will take over the management of the houses in addition to anything else I require of you. I will provide you with a housing allowance, a new car at each location, and a generous, separate clothing allowance. My wife will not be seen in the same outfit in public twice. Appearances are everything in my world."

He looked with approval at the dress Cass had sent to Andi's office. A pale teal silk that covered one shoulder, the body skimmed her torso before flaring into a full skirt that swirled just above her knees. Andi would have loved the dress if she'd been able to wear it for Perseus.

Perseus. What would he say when he heard she'd gone out to dinner with Angus? Would he understand that she'd been forced into it? Would he give her the chance to explain that she'd had no choice? Or would it be no big deal?

Maybe Perseus didn't care if she dated other men. Their relationship was so new she didn't even know if it qualified as a relationship. She did know that she didn't want him seeing other women. The thought of Perseus out with someone else sent a spike of jealousy through her and how foolish was that? She barely knew him.

"You're awfully quiet, my dear. Thinking about all those houses? I'll tell you about them over dinner." Angus reached over and patted Andi's knee. When he left his hand there she brushed it off. He chuckled and shook his head.

"You'll get used to the idea of becoming Mrs. Angus

Ames, I promise you. Let it go for now. Concentrate on this evening. I'm taking you to the very exclusive Alexander's for dinner. All you have to do is smile and enjoy your meal."

So, Angus wasn't even interested in getting to know her. Small talk was all that was required tonight. The knot in her chest loosened slightly. She knew how to smile and act in public when she didn't mean it. Angus was right about one thing–Cass had trained her well.

Alexander's was located above a small river town twenty minutes north of La Crosse. It sat atop a bluff and looked down on the town and the river like a king on a throne set above his subjects. Large plate glass windows fronted the entire west wall of Alexander's dining room. Pristine white tablecloths covered square tables set far enough apart to allow for private conversation. A pair of white tapers glowed at each table, enhancing the intimate ambience of the low lighting.

Most of the tables were already filled with diners speaking in hushed tones. Silverware occasionally clinked against a plate or soup bowl. It was exactly the type of restaurant that Andi hated most. She thought wistfully of the hamburger joint Perseus had taken her to the previous night. They'd sat shoulder to shoulder with strangers at the picnic table and the noise level had been high and boisterous.

"Good evening, Mr. Ames, it's a pleasure to see you again. Your requested table is waiting. Follow me please."

To Andi's surprise the maître d' led them across the dining room to a central table next to the windows. She had expected Angus to request one of the more private alcoves set around the sides of the dining room which would have been more intimate. She should have realized that he would want to be seen with her.

Angus placed a possessive hand at the back of Andi's

waist as they walked across the room. She wondered if he thought she might turn and run or if he was indicating to the room that she belonged with him.

She wanted to run. She hated that people were watching them, stopping their meals to speculate about them. She had intentionally worn her highest heels tonight and at least had the satisfaction of standing a good half foot taller than Angus. She saw him glance once at her shoes and knew that the height difference bothered him.

The small sense of victory didn't last long however. Angus had won and he knew it. She was having dinner with him despite refusing his invitations.

Angus waved off the menus the maître d' offered. He ordered their meal without asking Andi what she preferred to eat as well as a bottle of champagne. She watched him through half-lowered lids but didn't waste her breath arguing. This was exactly why she didn't like the man. She had sensed his arrogance and complete lack of consideration for others.

Placing her napkin on her lap she made several bland observations about the view and the dining room. Angus smiled and handed her a glass of champagne, proposing a toast to "us". For a brief moment she considered tossing the champagne into Angus's face, then she shrugged and drank it instead. She had always found public scenes distasteful.

Salads were served–romaine with cranberries, walnuts, and goat cheese. Andi asked about Angus's favorite sports teams and listened to his answers with a very small piece of her mind.

Was this what life married to Angus would be like, she wondered? Perpetual small talk and not being able to order her own meals? She couldn't remember ever being so bored.

The main course arrived–pork medallions in mustard

cream sauce with tiny carrots and herbed new potatoes. She ate mechanically without tasting anything and commented on the river traffic and the fine summer weather.

When dessert was served–tangy lemon sorbet and pistachio macarons–Cat, her mother's favored newspaper photographer/writer, showed up and took several shots of them.

Andi had been expecting Cat to show all evening. There was no way that her mother would pass up a chance to get a photo of one of the Whites into the paper. Her mother was a huge believer in publicity and had most likely called Cat to tell her where to find Angus and Andi.

Which meant of course that Angus had told her mother where they would be dining.

Angus covered her hand with his and smiled for the camera. Andi managed a small smile that felt more like a grimace and said nothing when Cat asked if there was romance in the air. Angus told Cat to watch for an announcement soon and Cat left with a satisfied grin on her face.

Andi's insides felt like a block of ice. Her meal sat heavy in her belly. She ignored her dessert and quit the pretense of small talk. "I'd like to go home now, if you don't mind. It's been a long week and I'm tired."

She heard her name called as they were leaving the restaurant and turned to her right. André Lightfoot sat alone at a table grinning at her. He stood and hurried over to her, kissing both her cheeks while Angus glowered at them both. Andi laughed at the handsome athlete.

"André, what a surprise. I didn't see you come in."

"And I didn't realize you were here until I saw the photographer. I smiled for her but unfortunately she only had eyes for you and your date."

He sighed dramatically and Andi grinned in response. She heard a throat clearing behind her and reluctantly turned.

"André, do you know Angus Ames? Angus is a business associate of my father's. Angus this is André Lightfoot, soccer player extraordinaire."

The two men shook hands. Angus placed a possessive hand on Andi's back and propelled her past André. "Excuse us but Andi needs to get home."

Andi allowed herself a brief eye roll. André winked at her and returned to his table.

Neither of them spoke until Angus pulled up to the curb in front of her condo. It was still fairly early, the evening gloaming just descending on the city. Small groups hung on the sidewalks in front of the many bars, the neon signs were lit, and music pulsed through the air from the bars and cruising cars.

Angus rounded the car to open the door for her but she beat him to it. He frowned at her as he grabbed her hand and pulled her from the car.

"In the future you will wait for me to get the door for you. You never know when someone will be watching."

Andi looked at him in surprise. "Do you always worry about what others think of you?" She hadn't expected that of him. Arrogance usually went hand in hand with not caring what others thought.

Angus frowned at her. "Of course I care. Image is every-thing. Which reminds me—you will never again wear heels when we are out in public. You are tall enough without them. Get rid of any you may have in your closet that are over two inches. I'll buy you new ones of the appropriate height."

For a long moment Andi simply stared at him in disbelief. "I'm surprised you want to marry a woman who is taller than you if that's the way you feel." She didn't try to hide the snark in her tone.

Angus took her elbow and propelled her toward her door. "I told you, you're the most beautiful woman I've ever met. Your elegant mother has trained you well. You impress people, and since I always insist on having the best of anything, in this case that happens to be you."

He didn't try to kiss her. Andi assumed that was because he'd have had to stand on his toes to reach her lips and even that would have been a stretch. The thought made her smile.

Andi unlocked the door and started to step inside but Angus stopped her with a hand on her arm.

"I've already booked a wedding planner and begun making the necessary arrangements. There's no reason we can't be married before the end of the month."

Andi's blood ran cold. "The end of the month is only two weeks away. You can't possibly put a wedding together that fast. I haven't even looked at dresses."

"You'll soon learn that if you throw enough money at something you can make whatever you want happen. Besides, your mother tells me she has already found your dress."

"Of course she has." Andi turned away and let herself in the door, wishing she could make it slam.

She felt so incredibly angry. Angry and frightened and physically ill.

# CHAPTER 19

UNLIKE THE PREVIOUS night when she'd waited for Perseus to drive away, Andi didn't wait for Angus to drive off before she headed up to her condo. She needed to put distance between them as quickly as possible.

She kicked off the heels as soon as she walked through her door. "Spoo-ook," she called out. "I'm home, cutie."

The kitten came skittering out of the bedroom to greet her with loud mews. Andi picked him up and buried her face in his fur. The kitten licked her chin with his tiny, rough tongue.

"What am I going to do, Spook? The man is a despicable human being. I can't bear the thought of being married to him. But I can't bear the thought of everyone who works for Dad losing their jobs. How could he let this happen? What a bloody mess."

She checked her cell phone which had been turned off all evening. She hadn't wanted to risk Perseus calling while she was out with Angus but she needn't have worried—there were no messages. More disappointed than relieved she undressed and put on her favorite ratty sweats. She'd been wearing them a lot these past two weeks, not a good sign as she usually reserved them for periods of emotional doldrums.

To say she was depressed was an understatement, she mused as she examined her feelings while she fed Spook. Twenty four hours before she'd been happier than she could ever have imagined. Now she was drowning in misery.

She stared at her phone when it rang, not quite ready to speak to Perseus. A quick peek at the screen showed it was only her mother. For a brief moment Andi considered letting it go to voice mail. Let her mother think she was still out with Angus. Common sense soon prevailed however.

If she knew her mother–and she believed she did–Cass and Angus would have already talked about tonight's date. If she didn't pick up her mother would certainly show up at the condo.

"Hello, Mother."

"Andi, dear."

As much as her mother ever allowed herself to sound enthusiastic, Andi could hear the delight in her voice.

"I just got off the phone with Angus and he's very pleased with how your dinner went this evening. He said you looked stunning and behaved with all the decorum he expects in a woman soon to be his wife. Of course I expected nothing less from you."

The smugness in her mother's voice made Andi's blood boil. She pulled the phone away from her ear and stared at it for a moment. Her mother was still speaking.

"He was not pleased with how you greeted Mr. Lightfoot, however. You will have to watch that inappropriate behavior in the future. I've known Angus for several years and I feel I should point out that he is possessive about what belongs to him."

"I'm not a possession, Mother. Nor do I belong to Angus Ames." Yet. She didn't belong to him *yet*. But she would unless some miracle occurred. Her meal sat like a lead ball in her belly.

"Semantics, Andromeda. This is very exciting. Your marriage to Angus will make both our companies powerhouses in the sports memorabilia world."

Andi wandered to the large windows and stared out at the lights strung across the blue bridges.

"In other words I'm a bargaining chip. You care so little about me then, Mother?" She felt close to tears. She pressed the heel of her free hand to her eyes.

"Of course I care about you." Cass sounded genuinely surprised by Andi's accusation. "I'm very proud of the beauty you've become. I'm the envy of all the mothers in my club."

A tug maneuvered a flotilla of barges under the two bridges. The barges rode high on the water, a sign that they were empty, heading north to the cities to be loaded with grain.

Her mother was proud of her beauty, something she had absolutely nothing to do with–an accident of fate. Had Cass ever been proud of the person Andi had become? She had worked hard all her life to be worthy of her mother's and father's love and pride. Look where it had gotten her.

If she'd been a rebellious daughter Angus Ames wouldn't have looked twice at her. He might have looked, she amended, but he definitely wouldn't want to marry her. It was precisely because she'd been so eager to please that he assumed she would be a malleable doormat of a wife.

And dammit, she had behaved like a doormat. Uselessly trying to trade good behavior for affection. Anger and shame at her neediness filled her.

A suspicion suddenly formed in Andi's mind.

"Why did you marry Dad, Mother?"

"What does that have to do with anything? Honestly Andromeda, what a question."

"It's a question I'd like an answer to. Did you love him? Do you love him now?"

Her mother was silent for several long moments, long enough for Andi to think she wasn't going to answer the question.

"There are more important things in life than love, Andromeda. You'll learn that soon enough. You should have learned it already. I've tried to set an example for you.

"Your father and I make a good team. We built Cepheus White Sports into the successful company it is today. My part behind the scenes was just as important as what your father handled. Social connections make the difference between moderate or huge success in life and I devoted my life to making those connections."

"So you never loved Dad," Andi said flatly. She wasn't surprised. She supposed that she'd always known it. She had never seen any physical affection between her parents. No spontaneous hugs or kisses or even a hand on a shoulder. She had always assumed that they were simply unwilling to show affection in front of their daughter, but she had also assumed that there *was* affection.

It hurt to know that if her mother never loved her father she certainly had no love for her daughter. It was too much on top of the evening she'd just had.

"I have to go, Mother. I'm tired." Tired of Cepheus White Sports, tired of her manipulating mother.

"Wait, we haven't discussed the wedding. I already picked out the perfect dress. You'll need to go in for a fitting in the next day or two. When will you see Angus again? I need to let Cat know. We don't want to miss any photo ops. We'll keep feeding the public until the big event and then splash that everywhere."

"You sound just like a public relations director. Good night, Mother."

Andi terminated the call. The thought of her mother's favorite gossip columnist following her around for the next two weeks made her shudder.

The phone rang again immediately. Her mother of course. Cass would hate that Andi had hung up on her. Too bad. She shut the phone off and tossed it on the couch, grabbed Spook and crawled into bed without changing out of her sweats.

She wanted to cry but had no tears. She felt angry and betrayed and filled with a dull ache that she couldn't identify. She fell asleep and dreamed of a big handsome man dressed in black leather who lifted her onto his iron horse like the knights of yore and spirited her away.

# CHAPTER 20

ANDI LEFT her phone turned off, deleting her Mother's increasingly angry messages. When her buzzer sounded she ignored that as well, watching from her window as Charles drove her mother away.

Perseus called her twice. She listened to his deep, smooth voice, then regretfully deleted his messages as well. There was no point in talking to him, it would only add to her misery. Besides, what could she tell him? That she was being sacrificed upon the marriage altar to an arrogant, manipulative man old enough to be her father?

It was better that Perseus think she wasn't interested. Unlike in her dream, Perseus couldn't help. And she knew he would try to help her because he was that kind of man—and there wasn't anything he could do to change the situation.

By Sunday afternoon she felt the need to get out of the condo so she took a walk around the historic district, checking out shop windows but with no desire to go into any of the stores.

"Andi! Andi, wait up!" André Lightfoot joined her on the sidewalk. His grin flashed as he tucked her hand through his arm. "It's my lucky day. I was headed to Sloppy's for a drink. Can I buy you one?"

Andi's first instinct was to refuse, but then she thought about the lonely evening that stretched ahead and changed her mind. She could use a distraction and some of the light-hearted banter André would provide.

"Thank you, André. I'd like that. You can tell me what you're up to and why you've been gracing La Crosse with your presence. You're usually here and gone."

"It's no big secret," he answered as he held the bar door open for her. "I've been teaching a class for a summer soccer program at the college geared for grade school kids. Several of my teammates are doing the same thing at other schools. I chose to teach here in La Crosse because I know my way around."

They settled at two high stools at the window bar looking out on the side street that ran by Sloppy's. Michelle the waitress came over to take their orders.

"IPA on tap?" she asked André.

"Yep. And my friend here will have–"

Michelle pointed her pen at Andi. "Mojito, right? I remember you from last week's happy hour."

Andi blushed. "I'd prefer a white wine today, thank you. Sauvignon Blanc if you have it."

"You come here often?" she asked after Michelle left to fill their orders. "The waitress knew what you wanted."

André shrugged. "It's comfortable, it's a sports bar, there's usually a good crowd. I like to be around people and I put off going back to the dorm as long as possible."

"You're staying in the dorms? Why not rent a place?"

He shrugged. "It's only for three weeks. Three camp groups, one week each. No big deal. The dorms are reasonably comfortable. I've slept in worse places."

Andi found herself relaxing with her wine and André's conversation. It felt natural to tell him about Angus Ames when he mentioned seeing them together Friday night at Alexander's restaurant. He was satisfyingly indignant about the situation.

"Have dinner with me tonight, Andi," he begged. "Don't make me eat alone. Any place you want to go. My treat." By then most of the tables and bar stools had filled. The music had been turned up and the noise level had risen. André tried to press another glass of wine on her when she regretfully passed on dinner but she told him she was ready to go home.

Andi made her escape while André was at the bar settling the tab. She knew it was a cowardly thing to do but she didn't want him to walk her home and she sensed that he intended to offer. She liked André and it had been nice of the soccer player to buy her a drink, but at some point in their conversation he'd made it clear that he'd like more from her.

He wasn't looking for something long term–she understood that André was a player and liked lots of women. But she wasn't interested in a fling of any duration, and because she honestly liked him she figured it was better to sneak away and avoid a confrontation. She would make her excuses another time.

The last time she'd walked home from Sloppy's she'd been drunk and Lauren had been with her. The next day Ashley was dead. Drowned. Or as Pandora suspected, the victim of a serial killer.

Andi fed Spook, made dinner for herself and went to bed early. She showered and dressed for work Monday morning–not in one of the dozens of power suits bought by her mother–but in jeans with a short sleeved pale blue linen blouse and white sneakers.

She worked on the seventh floor with customer service.

She didn't need to dress for the eighth floor. Her mother's adage about "dress for success" no longer applied. Nor did she feel her usual need to dress well because she was Cepheus White's daughter and had an image to uphold.

She slid some gold bangles on her left arm and added a beaded belt she especially loved. After some deliberation she decided to wear her hair in a simple French braid. She felt more comfortable walking to the office than she ever had.

Maybe she'd take all her power suits to a local church that collected business clothing for women who wanted better paying office jobs but couldn't afford the necessary wardrobes. The thought briefly buoyed her spirits.

Gus's eyebrows climbed nearly to his graying hairline when she came through the door. "Good morning, Miss Andromeda. I almost didn't recognize you."

"Is that a good thing or a bad thing, Gus?"

"Oh, it's a good thing, Miss. You're looking mighty fine today, if I may say so."

Andi smiled and thanked him. Her parents wouldn't approve of her clothing but at least someone did.

Maggie's eyebrows also climbed in surprise when she saw Andi but she was on a call so merely waved good morning and gave her a puzzled frown. It wasn't long however before she appeared at Andi's office door with Lauren right behind her.

"What's wrong?" Maggie demanded.

Andi looked up from her computer screen. "What makes you think something's wrong?"

The two women stepped inside the small office and with some maneuvering managed to close the door.

"I've watched you come to work every day for nearly three years." Maggie put her hands on her hips. "Never once in all that time have you worn jeans to the office. Something's wrong. Spill. We're here to help."

Three bodies in her cramped office was two bodies too many. Add the closed door and Andi felt as if all the air had been sucked from the room. She frowned at the women but it was obvious they weren't going anywhere until they got what they wanted.

Why not tell them? She suddenly felt the need to tell someone. Her shoulders sagged and she slumped back in her seat.

"I went on a dinner date Friday night with a man I've been refusing to date," she began.

Lauren's eyebrows bunched together. "Why on earth would you do that?"

"If you give me a chance I'll tell you."

Lauren rolled her hand in the universal "get on with it" signal.

"Right. Turned out this man wants to marry me. Not because he loves me but because he believes I'll be an asset to his business and make him handsome little heirs to his business kingdom. The wedding is in less than two weeks. He's already hired a wedding planner and my mother bought a dress for me to wear."

Both women were frowning at her now. Maggie shook her head. "Your mother bought you a wedding dress? Are you both crazy? You can't jump from one dinner date to marriage. That's . . . insane. No offense to you and your mother," she finished lamely, "but why would you agree to marry him? Why not date for a while?"

Andi curled her lip. "Oh, I think in this case my mother deserves your offense. The man's company is Cepheus White Sports' largest–and apparently now the only–supplier of clothing for monogramming and screen printing."

"Oh-oh. I think I see where this is going." Lauren's large blue eyes didn't look happy.

"If you're thinking the man threatened to shut the company down by withholding product unless I marry him you'd be right." Andi waited a beat. "So I had dinner with him Friday night–not knowing about the marriage bit then–and he's worse than I had imagined."

"Old and ugly?" Maggie looked sympathetic.

Andi shrugged one shoulder. "He's not terribly old and he's tolerably handsome in a plastic kind of way I guess. But he's absolutely controlling. He wants a wife who'll make small talk and run his five mansions and throw parties and shop for clothes and he's convinced I'd be perfect."

"A lot of women would think they'd hit the mega-million lottery with that offer," Lauren pointed out. "I know it's sudden but are you sure this is a bad thing?"

She should have known they wouldn't understand. "Never mind. I really need to get back to work."

Neither women budged.

Maggie leaned her hands on the desk top. "You don't strike me as a woman who would agree to marriage after only one date. Help us understand why you're doing this."

"I don't *want* to marry this man. I want a family with a man I love who loves me in return. I don't want my parents' kind of marriage." She lifted a hand and let it fall into her lap. "I don't want a marriage that's nothing more than a business arrangement. If I marry this man any chance I have at happiness will disappear and I'll grow into a bitter old woman," she added quietly.

"Then don't marry him. Simple."

Andi looked at Lauren. "Simple? Weren't you *listening*? If I don't marry Angus Ames everyone who works for Cepheus White Sports will lose their jobs in less than a month."

She nodded at the shocked expressions on Maggie's and Lauren's faces. Obviously they hadn't understood what having no product meant to the company.

"Now you get it," she continued, satisfied that they finally understood the situation. "Dad will have no choice but to shut down the company. He can't set up a new supply chain quick enough to compensate for losing Ames's partnership and the company can't afford to keep paying idle workers. So you see, I'm stuck. If I tell Angus Ames to take a flying leap you both will lose your jobs. As well as over five hundred other employees."

She thought about Gus and his smile whenever he saw her. Gus was too old to go job hunting. She knew there were many more Gus's in the company. Workers with only basic education and limited skills. Being thrust onto the job market would be a tremendous hardship for them.

"I can't be responsible for so many losing their jobs."

"There must be another way." Maggie's face had paled beneath the light sunburn she'd acquired over the weekend.

Andi knew Maggie and Lauren were among those who couldn't afford to lose their jobs. No one who worked for the company could. Only the higher salaried employees, mainly the ones who worked on the eighth floor, made enough to maybe have a cushion while they looked for a new job. The majority survived from paycheck to paycheck. They had families to support, car payments, insurance, mortgages, dreams to fund.

The sacrifice of one for the good of many. There was no other way. She sighed.

"Thanks for checking on me. I appreciate it, I really do, but I'll be fine. I just need to wrap my head around it, that's all. Now I really need to get back to work."

She left her office door closed the remainder of the day.

She couldn't handle any more sympathy and she didn't want to discuss the situation again, even with well meaning friends.

Fortunately her father didn't call her to his office. Andi didn't think she could face him until she re-established her personal defenses, and even then she wasn't sure she'd want anything to do with her parents ever again.

She took the stairs down to street level at the end of the workday, avoiding the elevator and any possibility of running into Maggie or Lauren. She appreciated their concern but talking about the situation only made her feel worse than she already felt.

The sidewalks were filled with people headed home from their jobs or out for a bite to eat or an after work drink. Couples and parents with children of all ages gawked at store windows or the architecture of La Crosse's historic district. The food trucks did a healthy business and the sidewalk tables outside restaurants were filling with happy people.

Snatches of lively conversations washed over her. Andi loved the vibrant small city even though she'd spent most of her life away at the various boarding schools her parents had sent her to.

She turned the corner onto her street. Her heart lurched when she saw a familiar figure leaning against her building beside the door. She almost turned around. She *would* have turned around if he hadn't already seen her, but he had so she kept walking toward him.

"Have you been avoiding me, Andromeda?" Piercing green eyes searched her face. "We need to talk."

# CHAPTER 21

ANDI TRIED to act cool but very much doubted her success. The truth was she was thrilled to see Perseus again, even if he represented a complication she didn't need in her life right now. For some reason she had assumed that he would simply forget about her if she ignored his calls. The fact that he hadn't, that he wanted to see her enough to track her down, warmed her heart.

"Avoiding you?" Andi tried to smile. "Why would I do that?" God he looked good standing there in his favored old khakis with grass stains on the knees and hips, his arms crossed over his broad chest as he continued to lean against the building.

Perseus's eyes glittered with amusement. "Well now, I was wondering that very thing. Why would Andromeda avoid me? I asked myself. Was the hamburger joint I took her to too downscale for her taste?"

He waited a moment. When Andi didn't say anything he answered his own question. "No, I don't think that's it. She seemed to enjoy her meal. So. Was it the motorcycle when she's used to fancy cars?"

His eyes remained locked on hers while he waited a beat. One corner of his mouth lifted. "I definitely had the feeling that she was enjoying herself. I don't think the bike was a problem."

Andi looked away and put her key into the lock. "I had a wonderful time with you," she said softly. *Don't be a coward, look at him.*

She lifted her head and focused on the small triangle of chest hair curling from the open neck of his polo shirt. The urge to reach out and touch it made her hand shake. She gripped her tote tighter to hide it.

"Okaaay." Perseus reached out a hand and gently lifted her chin, forcing her to look him in the eyes. The compassion she saw there brought tears to her own. She blinked furiously to get rid of them but she knew he had seen them. He let go of her chin and reached around her to open the door.

"Let's go upstairs and talk," he said, taking her arm and propelling her into the small lobby.

Andi didn't protest. She unlocked her mailbox, grabbed the mail, and let them both into the stairwell.

"Why don't you ever use the elevator?"

"I do when I have too much to carry up three flights. The stairs are part of my exercise routine. And to be honest I'm a little claustrophobic. The elevator feels like a trap. I read about a power outage in Manhattan once. Over eight hundred elevators were stuck until the lights came back on. I'm not sure I'd survive that experience."

She was intensely aware of Perseus climbing the stairs behind her, close enough that she could feel the heat from his body. Her heart began to beat faster. She cast around for something to say.

"How did your business trip go? Chicago, wasn't it?"

Making small talk was her fallback in situations where she was bored or nervous. She definitely wasn't bored at the moment and she had no reason to be nervous, she scolded herself. Only she did. She so did.

"The business trip went very well except for the fact that the woman I happen to be crazy about refused to take my calls."

"Oh." He was crazy about her. The knowledge made her want to cry. She let them into the condo where they were immediately greeted by Spook who arched his back at the sight of Perseus before realizing who it was. Then he mewed loudly and rubbed against Perseus's ankle.

Perseus reached down and engulfed the tiny kitten in one large hand. "Hello little guy. You've grown since I saw you last." He settled the kitten against his neck and looked at Andi. "I imagine you need to feed him before we talk."

Andi could only nod in reply. The lump in her throat had grown at the sight of the gentle way Perseus handled Spook. She tossed down her tote and hurried into the kitchen area to put some distance between them.

Perseus took her hand as soon as she set food and fresh water down for Spook and led her to the couch. He pulled her down beside him, keeping his hold on her hand and turning to face her.

"Okay, tell me what's going on. And don't say 'nothing', because you and I both know that whatever is bothering you is serious. And just so you don't try to spare me the details I should tell you that Pandora's friend Maggie came to see her today."

Andi started. "Pandora knows Maggie Hoffmann?"

"Yes. Apparently they've become good friends since they met at a school fund raiser for one of Sam's kid's schools last year."

"She–she told Pandora about Angus Ames?" It hadn't occurred to Andi that Maggie or Lauren would tell someone else about her situation. She should have thought of that before she shared with them. Unfortunately it was too late now.

She took a deep breath and let it out. "I shouldn't have said anything to them."

"Why not? Maggie's worried about you. What your parents and Ames are doing to you is despicable and archaic."

"I know. But I don't see what choice I have. I can't let all those people lose their jobs, Percy."

"I agree."

Andi's body turned cold with despair. Even Perseus could see that she had no choice but to marry Angus Ames. She tried to pull her hand free but he held on tighter.

"I agree that you can't let all those people lose their livelihood," he told her, "but I don't agree that you should marry Ames. In fact I emphatically *dis*agree with that course of action."

Andi gave her head a slight shake and closed her eyes. "I don't have any choice, Percy. I think you'd better go." She tried to free her hand again. This time Perseus scooped her onto his lap and wrapped his arms around her. She tried to resist but it felt too good to be held and comforted. To her dismay she began to cry and she couldn't stop.

"Shhhh, sweetheart, it's going to be all right," Perseus told her as he stroked her hair and back. He felt a great deal of anger and contempt toward the people who were hurting this beautiful woman and fully intended to rectify the situation. But first she had to trust him and tell him what she wanted.

Andi kept her face buried in his chest until her sobs

slowed. "I'm so embarrassed," she hiccuped. "I got your shirt all wet."

Perseus wiped the tears from her cheeks with his thumb and kissed her forehead. "Not a problem."

He kissed her temples, then her cheeks. "You can cry on me any time, Andromeda."

Finally he moved to her mouth. He knew his timing was bad but he couldn't resist. She was so damn beautiful and unlike most beautiful women she seemed unaware of how her beauty affected others. Andromeda White was a genuinely warm and caring person and he found her irresistible. The thought of her married to another man was intolerable. She belonged with him.

He deepened the kiss, teasing her lips open so he could sweep his tongue inside and taste her. She made a small moan deep in her throat and wrapped her arms around his neck, holding him closer. When he felt her tongue tentatively reach inside his mouth he groaned and splayed one hand on the back of her head to hold her there.

Heat flamed between them. Perseus broke the kiss and pressed his forehead to Andi's. "I want you," he said, his voice rough. "But I don't want to take advantage of your emotional state. You were right, I think I'd better leave while I still can."

The last thing he wanted to do was leave Andromeda.

Andi's arms tightened on his neck. Her body felt tingly and inflamed and all she could think of was pressing closer to the magnificent man who held her. The man who already held her heart even though she'd only known him a short while.

If she was going to spend her life married to a cold bastard named Angus Ames then she wanted to experience love making at least once the way it should be between two people .

"Please don't go," she whispered against his lips. "I want you to make love to me." When he didn't move and didn't answer she thought he was going to refuse her. *"Please,"* she begged. "I want my first time to be with you, not–not . . . him."

"Are you sure?" Perseus could barely get the words out he was so caught up in his need for her. He felt her nod and right or wrong he knew he didn't have the strength to walk out. He stood with her in his arms and carried her back to the bedroom.

The bedroom was uncluttered, like the rest of the condo. It contained a king sized bed with a bowed, spindled head-board in cherry and a low, six drawer cherry dresser. A jungle of plants filled the windows that looked on the same view as the living room windows. A large, life sized oil painting of a shaggy Highland cattle hung on the wall oppo-site the walk-in closet.

Perseus laid Andi on the bed and removed her sneakers. She reached up and grabbed his belt, pulling him down on top of her. He was careful to support his weight on his fore-arms so he didn't crush her.

"Last chance to change your mind," he said as he placed a trail of kisses down the silky skin of her neck, all the while praying that she wouldn't change her mind.

"I've never wanted anything more than I want this," she told him as she bent her head to expose more of her neck for him. Every kiss he laid on her sent sparks of heat through her body. "I'm not going to change my mind."

"Good." A wicked gleam came into Perseus's eyes that made Andi's tummy do flip flops.

Perseus took his time, making sure that Andi was ready for him. He paid attention to every bit of her body, returning again and again to the places that were especially sensitive to his ministrations. He wasn't surprised to discover that she was an eager learner and a passionate lover who did her best to give as much as she received.

They were both bathed in a sheen of sweat and panting for breath when they finally collapsed in a tangled heap. It had grown dark outside and the bridge lights shone between the leaves of her plants.

"I had no idea," Andi said when her breathing finally evened out. If she had known how glorious sex with Perseus would be she never would have gone through with it, she thought sadly. How could she ever allow Angus Ames to touch her now that she knew how wonderful lovemaking should be?

She tried to pull away but Perseus tightened his arm around her. She lay half on top of him, their legs still tangled. "I should get cleaned up," she told him. She was afraid if she laid with him any longer she might never want to leave and she couldn't let that happen.

"And you really should go," she added.

"We still haven't talked."

"But you know everything already. You said Maggie talked to Pandora. What's left to talk about?"

Perseus lifted her chin so he could look into those mesmerizing blue eyes. "We need to talk about what we're going to do so you don't have to marry Angus Ames."

Andi struggled to get free. "There's nothing to be done," she said flatly. "I really think you'd better leave now."

While Perseus dressed he had argued that they could find a solution to her situation but she had refused to listen. He didn't understand. Too many people would be adversely affected if she didn't go through with the wedding to Angus.

After she closed and locked the condo door behind him

Andi listened to the sound of his footsteps fade as he entered the stairwell. Only then did she allow the tears to flow.

Perseus stood outside Andi's building and took several deep breaths to gain control over the stew of emotions flowing through him. Anger at Andromeda's parents and Angus, frustration that she wouldn't let him try to help her, satisfaction over what had taken place between them a short while before all warred for his attention.

After several minutes he turned east and headed back to his brother's place to talk things over with Zee. He never noticed the car sitting halfway up the block, its lone occupant watching the entrance to the condo building.

# CHAPTER 22

ANDI PLAYED hooky from work the next day, something she had never before done. She felt guilty because she wasn't sick at all–at least not physically ill–but she felt heartsick and unable to face Maggie or Lauren. She knew the women would both try to speak with her about her upcoming marriage and she couldn't bear to talk about it.

She also feared that she might tell them about Perseus. Making love with him had opened her eyes to the magical potential that two people could share and had left her feeling vulnerable. She had wanted to call him back as soon as she made him leave.

Unfortunately the person she had to notify was her father's admin assistant, Spencer. She could have sworn she heard him sniff with disapproval.

She also should have anticipated that word would get back to her father and that her father would then call her Mother. Cass called not ten minutes after Andi's brief conversation with Spencer.

Andi tapped her fingers on the counter next to her phone and debated answering. She hadn't spoken to her mother since hanging up on her Friday night after the date with Angus. It amazed her that she didn't feel the least bit guilty about hanging up on her mother.

Spook distracted her from the ringing phone. He was trying to climb the leg of her sweatpants as he insisted on having attention. His little needle sharp claws were pricking holes in her calf. She plucked him from her leg and settled him on her lap which was exactly what the little guy wanted. His golden yellow eyes blinked at her and he began to purr with satisfaction.

The phone stopped ringing. Andi immediately listened to her mother's message.

"Andromeda White, you pick up this phone or I'll come over there and disturb everyone in the building until someone lets me in."

Andi knew it wasn't an idle threat. Cass thought nothing of inconveniencing others if it got her something she wanted. The phone rang again. Andi gave in with a heavy sigh and answered.

"Hello, Mother. What do you want?"

"That's a fine way to greet your mother. I've been trying to reach you for days. We have a great deal to accomplish before the wedding–which is only ten days from now, I might add."

Andi doodled absently on the pad of paper she kept on the counter for memos or her shopping lists. She made a note to contact the church to see who she should call about the business suits she wanted to donate for their Women to Work program.

"Andi? Are you listening? I have the guest list drawn up and the wedding planner that Angus hired wants to sit down with both of us as soon as possible. I told her we could meet with her this afternoon. Unfortunately we won't be able to have the lavish ceremony you deserve because of the short notice, but we'll get as much exposure and publicity as possible.Fortunately I notified the people who matter to save the date back when Angus first approached me. You also need to swing by the dress shop for a fitting although I suspect very little will need to be done. I've bought enough clothing for you over the years that I know what will fit."

Andi doodled some more. Angus had told her that he didn't want her to wear her high heels any more so she should probably donate her shoes as well. Although now that she was thinking about them, her shoes were all top quality and pricey and all one size. Perhaps a better plan would be to sell them and donate the proceeds to a shoe fund so the women could buy their own shoes instead.

"Andi." Cass's voice sounded sharp. "I'll have Charles pick you up at quarter to two. The wedding planner will be here at two. Dress professionally. We want to make a good impression."

Andi ended the call without saying a word and turned off the phone. She'd hung up on her mother twice in as many calls she realized with surprise. Her mother wouldn't like that one little bit.

An even bigger surprise was that Andi finally understood that she'd spent her life trying to win the love and approval of a woman she didn't even like. The knowledge left her somewhat breathless and a little shaky. A child should love her parents.

But then, a child should be freely given love by her parents and not feel that she had to earn it.

She needed to get out of her condo. She needed to move and she needed to think. She cupped Spook to her chest and went into the bedroom to change into shorts and a tee shirt. She pulled on her sneakers, put some cash and her keys into her pocket and placed Spook into his carrier, then set off too see Pandora and Sam. She needed to be around people who understood and cherished family.

She almost turned back when she reached Pandora's driveway and remembered that Perseus might be there, but her need to see the two women and the children drove her forward.

The sounds of a whiffle ball game drew her to the back yard. To her relief, Zee and Perseus weren't playing. The kids shouted her name and ran to greet her, all talking at once except for Ariel who merely babbled and smiled at her.

Andi handed Spook's carrier to Danny who loved the kitten and would take care of him and scooped Ariel into her arms, giving the beautiful little girl a kiss on the cheek. Ariel laughed and patted Andi's cheeks with two pudgy, dirt-stained hands.

"You're just in time," Pandora called to her. "We're playing family against family and I'm outgunned. You're part of my family now so you get to play on my team."

Just like that all the tension drained from Andi's body. She knew that Pandora didn't mean that she was actually part of the family but the words were still a balm on her troubled soul.

Sam's kids were all athletic and obviously had a lot of practice at whiffle ball. Andi found that she didn't have to hold back in fear of overpowering them and she played hard for the next hour, coaching six year old Greg with his batting and carrying a giggling Ariel around the bases with her. They were all hot and sweaty and grass stained when they agreed to call the game a draw.

Pandora's four year old Mia and Sam's seven year old Sarah each grabbed one of Andi's hands and pulled her into the kitchen with the others for lemonade and cookies. Andi allowed herself to be coerced into sharing refreshments and sat at the table chatting with the children until Sam shooed them up to the playroom for some quiet time.

"Quiet time for us, not them," she told Andi with a laugh.

After the children departed the women moved to the comfortable chairs next to the fireplace. Ariel climbed into her mother's lap and promptly fell asleep. Spook and Squirt were already napping together in Squirt's cat bed by the fireplace.

"It appears that we have a mutual friend," Pandora began.

Andi made a wry expression. "Apparently. I assume you mean Maggie?"

"Yes. She left work early yesterday and came by. She feels terrible about what your parents are doing to you."

"Not as bad as I feel, believe me." Andi shook her head and shrugged one shoulder. "I don't see that I have any choice in the matter, Pandora. How can I let all those people lose their jobs? Cepheus White Sports isn't the largest employer in La Crosse by any means but we're a significant employer. Closing our doors would affect hundreds–if not thousands of people if I count the families."

"I understand what you're saying but there has to be something that can be done. I can't stand by and allow such an outrage to happen to someone I care about."

Sam nodded her agreement. "You aren't alone in this, Andi. We want to help."

The fierceness in Pandora's voice and the women's desire to help brought tears to Andi's eyes. She seemed to be crying far too easily these days. If she lived in Regency times she'd be called a watering pot, and rightly so.

"Thank you. I appreciate that you want to help, but I think Angus Ames and my mother have boxed me into a corner." Searching her brain for a change of subject she hit on one.

"Have you learned any more about your suspected serial killer?" she asked.

"Yes." Pandora shifted Ariel to the couch and sat back down. "I found similar drownings in Milwaukee, Winona, and Madison. In each one the victim was young, pretty, and had been last seen drinking at a local bar. Your friend Ashley was the twelfth in a string of "accidental" deaths over the last six years." She made air quotes around accidental.

"Twelve drownings? I don't understand why the police aren't looking for a serial killer." Andi couldn't believe so many young women had drowned without someone questioning their deaths. She found it frightening that a killer could operate so easily under the radar.

Before Pandora could speak again Luke came into the kitchen dressed in a baseball uniform and kissed Sam on the cheek. "I'm off, Mom. I'll be home for dinner. 'Bye Aunt Pan, 'bye Andi. You play pretty good ball–for a girl." His brown eyes sparkled at her.

"Gee, thanks." Andi couldn't help but smile at the handsome teen. "Next time I'll show no mercy."

Luke laughed and left.

"He's a nice kid. You must be very proud of him," Andi told Sam.

"I am. He's not really a kid anymore though. My Luke is almost a man."

"The teenage girls are already storming the castle," Pandora told Andi, laughing. "And in a few more years it will be Zack's turn and then Danny's. At least I'll know what to expect by the time my own kids start dating."

Sam and Pandora grinned at each other. Andi envied their closeness and yet instinctively knew that for whatever reasons, these two women were willing to welcome her into their family circle.

Pandora turned serious. "So, back to why the police haven't caught on to our killer." She took a sip of her lemonade and sat back in her chair. "I found twelve drownings–including Ashley's–in four locations over six years. All in late spring or summer. The drownings look like accidents and are spread out every two years or so in each locale so the police haven't thought to link them. The La Crosse and Winona drownings all took place in late June, the others in July.

"They assume, and not unreasonably, that the victims had too much to drink and either fell in the rivers or went swimming."

"Are the . . . bodies always found in rivers?" Andi asked.

"Yes." Pandora ticked them off on her fingers. "The Yahara in Madison, the Milwaukee River in Milwaukee, and the Mississippi in La Crosse and Winona. There've been three drownings in each location."

"So the killer gets around, but the distances aren't that great. Madison is only two hours from here, Winona under an hour, and Milwaukee five, maybe six hours," Sam pointed out. "He could live in any of the four cities or somewhere else entirely. He might come to the area only in the summers."

"In other words, finding him unless he's caught in the act will be next to impossible." Andi shuddered. "And he might still be in the area."

"True. But he's already killed here this year. The police would take a hard look at another suspicious death so soon after Ashley's so I doubt he'll strike again. Hi, honey." Pandora gave a little wave and a brilliant smile as her husband walked into the kitchen from the mudroom.

Zee. Andi froze, her heartbeat sounding loud as a drum in

her chest. She shouldn't have stayed so long. Perseus was bound to be with his brother and she didn't think she could bear to see him.

Not until she had a chance to rebuild her armor against him.

As soon as she had the thought she dismissed it. Guarding against her feelings for Perseus was an impossible feat. The safest course of action was to stay away from him. She set down her glass and stood.

"I should get going."

Zee kissed his wife on the lips and straightened. His gray eyes searched Andi's face. "Sit down, Andi. There's no need for you to run off. You're family and we take care of our own."

That was the second time she'd been referred to as family that day. What had Perseus told his brother and Pandora? Andi felt her cheeks flame with embarrassment.

When she remained standing Zee put a large hand on her shoulder and gently pressed her back down into the chair. "*Sit.* Perseus isn't here. He had to fly back to Chicago this morning to deal with a client. I want to talk to you."

It wasn't a request. Zee expected her to obey him. Andi briefly debated leaving just to show Zee that she couldn't be bossed around, but realized she really didn't want to leave.

"Fine. What do you want to speak with me about?"

He sat on the arm of Pandora's chair and considered Andi.

"My half brother is a good man. Maybe the best of us if I'm going to be honest, although if you tell him I said that I'll deny it." He smiled, then grew serious again. "You have a problem and need our help."

Andi shook her head. "I appreciate your concern—I really

do—but there's nothing anyone can do to change the situation."

This time Zee's smile made Andi catch her breath. She couldn't look away from his eyes. He radiated power.

"Never doubt the determination of the gods when we set our minds to something, Andi. We may not rule the earth like we did millennia ago but we still wield a great deal of power, even if it's in a more modern form. Now tell me everything."

"Gods? Come on. That seems rather . . . egotistical of you."

She looked at Sam and Pandora. They were both smiling at her like the joke was on her. Zee's gaze held steady.

"You aren't kidding, are you? You're really a god?" Dear lord, did that mean Perseus was a god as well? She felt panic rise in her chest.

"Zeus is my father. And Percy's. His mother was a mortal so Percy is technically a demigod. We keep a low profile these days, but like I said, we still wield a great deal of power. So . . . you need our help."

PERSEUS HADN'T BEEN happy about making the unscheduled trip to Chicago. The owner of the company he was currently working with needed a lot of hand holding the closer they got to the final hurdles and had called that morning in a panic.

Under normal circumstances Perseus didn't mind doing the coddling. He understood how hard people worked to bring their dreams to life and how devastating it could be when they came close to losing those dreams.

Some businesses couldn't be saved. Either the owners waited too long to ask for help or they intentionally bled their companies of all their assets. Perseus walked away from those companies. He helped only those people who sincerely wanted help and were willing to do the work and make the necessary changes and sacrifices no matter how difficult.

He had to wonder if Cepheus White was willing to do whatever it took to get his company out from under Angus Ames's power.

He should have been concentrating all of his attention on the Chicago problem but thoughts of Andromeda kept intruding. Truth be told, she had filled his mind from the moment he'd seen her less than elegant exit from the elevator at her father's recent gala.

She was the one.

She was the one he wanted at his side, the one he wanted to marry til death do them part, the one he wanted to sire his children with. The way she had given herself to him the previous night had cemented his belief that she was meant for him. She had held nothing back and in return he had given her his heart.

Wisely, he had not told her that of course. And he wouldn't, not until he knew how she felt about him.

Yes, Andromeda White was the one. Unfortunately her family had put her on the auction block and sold her to another.

Perseus debarked the plane, met with the business owner and reassured him that all would be well, patiently going over all the steps they had before them to make his company solvent again, and then hopped another flight back to La Crosse to deal with his own crises. Under normal circumstances he would stick with the business owner until the turnaround was completed, but knowing Andromeda was in trouble changed everything.

He drove back to Pan and Zee's only to learn that she'd been there most of the day. He'd only missed her by a half hour.

Zee sat him down to discuss Andi's situation but Perseus couldn't concentrate. His need to see Andi kept distracting him.

"Percy! What the devil is wrong with you?" Zee frowned at his brother. "Pay attention. We need to come up with a strategy here and we don't have much time."

"I know, I know," Perseus muttered. He tried to focus

until he couldn't stand it any longer. The need to see Andi had become an overwhelming obsession. He jumped to his feet and headed to the back door. "I'm taking the bike." And he was gone, leaving Zee to stare after his brother with a puzzled frown.

Andi was thoughtful on her walk home after her conversation with Zee. She felt touched and humbled that Perseus's family had so readily embraced her. They sincerely wanted to help her.

She slid the straps of her tote higher on her shoulder and switched Spook's cat carrier to her other hand. Fortunately she didn't have to walk by her parents' house to get back to her condo. She wondered if the wedding planner had shown up and if she and Cass had proceeded to make plans without her. Her phone was probably melting with blistering messages from her mother.

The thought almost made her smile, but the knowledge that there would soon be a showdown between herself and her mother turned the smile to a grimace.

The day had turned midsummer hot, making her thankful for the city's tree-lined streets. She walked in the shade, hurrying across the sunny intersections, and crossing only when she met up with the occasional dog walker.

La Crosse was a pedestrian friendly city with bike paths which kept the cyclists off the well-maintained sidewalks. Between boarding schools and summer camps she hadn't had any opportunities growing up to really learn the city so she took advantage of her walks now to learn the neighborhoods she passed through.

The sidewalks became more crowded the nearer she

drew to the historic district and the river. The streets were lined with parked cars and people walked three and four abreast, forcing her to skirt around the groups. The sidewalk cafés were busy. Heavy bass blasted from a passing car filled with young men. Out on the river she could see the La Crosse Queen, a replica of the paddle wheelers that used to ply the river, its deck filled with passengers.

Summer was in full swing. Where would she be at this time next year? Planning a party at one of Angus's mansions? Clothes shopping in New York?

She shook off the depressing thoughts. The reality would be on her soon enough. There was no point in trying to imagine it.

"Andi! Andromeda! Wait up!"

Andi turned and found André bearing down on her, winding his way through the tourists with a smile and "excuse me"s. She waited for him to catch up to her.

"Where you headed?" he asked.

"I was on my way home. How did your soccer practice go today?" They turned and began to walk together.

"Great. I have one or two promising athletes in the last group, but then it's always that way. I was on my way to Sloppy's for a beer. Join me?"

"Thanks, but I can't." Andi lifted Spook's carrier. "I need to get the little guy home."

André gave her a pleading look. "Please," he wheedled. "Don't make me drink alone. It's such a pathetic thing to do. Save me from being pathetic. Please. One drink. That's all."

Andi laughed and relented. "One drink only. Then I have to scoot."

"Great. Here let me take that." He took the cat carrier from her hand and laced his fingers with hers. "So, tell me about your day. That's unusual attire for the office."

They found a free table in the back at Sloppy's and André went up to the bar to get Andi a white wine and himself a beer. Andi set Spook's carrier on an empty chair and tried to relax. Now that they were in Sloppy's she realized she didn't want to be there. She really wanted to get home after being out all day. And Spook needed to eat.

"I can't stay long," she reminded André when he returned with their drinks.

"I know. I get it. Drink up and I'll let you go. I just needed company for one beer, promise." He took his seat and smiled.

Andi made an effort to relax. Surely she could spare the time to keep André company for one drink. Besides, she'd always found him to be entertaining and pleasant to look at. She chatted and sipped at her drink–maybe a little faster than usual because she really wanted to get home–and was surprised to realize she felt dizzy when she stood.

"Whew! I might have drunk that a little too fast," she said, surprised by how drunk she felt. André's eyes filled with concern. "Hang on." He threw some bills on the table and took her arm.

Andi leaned on him. She was plastered. She'd never had a single glass of wine hit her so hard. It took her two tries to get her arm in the tote handles and pull it up to her shoulder. "Shpook," she slurred.

André smiled at her. "No problem. I've got your cat. Come on, let's get you home." He put his arm around Andi's waist and led her out of the busy bar, immediately turning down the side street that ran down toward the river.

Andi was having trouble holding her head up. It kept falling forward. She felt incredible embarrassed that André should see her in this condition. She wanted to apologize for inconveniencing him but her tongue wouldn't cooperate.

A small niggling thought tried to worm its way to the

front of her mind but she couldn't quite grasp it. It wasn't until she realized they were walking on a long stretch of grass that it became clear.

"This . . . isn't . . . home." Where were they? Something sparkled in front of her. Water. It was so hard to think clearly. She heard André chuckle close to her ear.

"No, my dear Andromeda, this isn't your quaint little condo. But you could say that it's about to become your home since it's the last place you will ever see."

What was he saying? This wasn't her condo. She couldn't think. Nothing made any sense.

André dropped the cat carrier and led Andi down to the bank of the river. They were at the southern end of the river park. It was quiet there as most visitors preferred the northern half of the park with its International Garden, the museum and paddle wheeler, and the benches for sitting that lined the river. The southern tip of the park was wild and secluded.

"Before you leave us Andromeda perhaps you'd like to know why I'm doing this? I can tell you because you'll never remember. The Rohypnol I put in your wine will blot out most of your memory. Not that it matters since you'll be dead anyway. Just another sleazy woman who drank too much and drowned. Such a pity."

Andi struggled to focus on the words. Rohypnol? André had given her the date rape drug? Why?

# CHAPTER 24

Perseus drove to Andi's condo building first. When she didn't answer her buzzer he assumed she had heard Zee's bike and was avoiding him. The thought didn't please him. He needed to see for himself that she was all right.

He rang the buzzers to the other five condos in the building until someone let him in. Taking the stairs two at a time to her floor, he knocked loudly on her door. "Andi? It's Percy. Let me in. I need to talk to you."

There was no answer. He listened for a long minute but the condo felt empty.

Perseus pulled out his phone and called her, but the call went straight to voice mail. "Andi, it's Percy. Call me as soon as you can. I'm worried about you."

Where could she be? She had Spook with her. Surely she wouldn't shop while carrying a cat. The feeling that something was wrong grew stronger. He raced back down the stairs and stood outside while he tried to guess where she might have gone.

Andi's world in La Crosse was pretty small, encompassing her work, the park where she liked to run, and the grocery store. In the last two weeks that world had expanded to include Sloppy's and Pandora's and Zee's.

She was on foot. She couldn't have gone far.

He could eliminate the office since it was past office hours. And his brother's place since he had just come from there. And while he knew from his research that Cepheus White lived next door to Zee he felt certain that Andi hadn't gone there–her emotions were still too raw from the way her parents had used her.

That left Sloppy's and the park. Sloppy's was between Zee's and Andi's condo and therefore the most likely place for her to be so he'd start there.

He decided against taking the bike since parking in the historic district could be a problem and jogged up to the sports bar instead, all the while railing against the time it took. A quick word with the waitress informed him that Andi had indeed been there earlier with the good looking soccer player whose name she couldn't remember.

What really disturbed Perseus was the news that Andi had staggered out of the place leaning heavily on her companion. Had she been taken ill? Had the soccer player taken her to the hospital? Maybe that was why he felt this pending sense of doom weighing on him.

He stood on the sidewalk in front of Sloppy's, oblivious to the fact that he was blocking a large portion of the side-walk and forcing the tourists to part around him.

Where was she?

Perseus whipped out his phone and punched in Zee's number. "I can't find Andi. What kind of shape was she in when she left the house?"

"She was fine, Percy, why?"

"The waitress at Sloppy's said she was here with some

soccer bloke and she could barely stagger out of the place after one glass of wine. That doesn't sound like Andi."

Zee was silent for a long moment. "I agree. You checked her condo?"

"Yeah. She wasn't there. I'm headed down to the park. Something's wrong, Zee. I can feel it."

"Right. I'll meet you at the park."

Perseus thanked the gods that his brother took his bad feeling seriously. "Thanks, Zee. Start at the north end. I'll search the south end where she usually runs and we'll meet in the middle. Hopefully one of us will find her." He shut off the phone and slipped it in his pocket, then sprinted back to Andi's condo to pick up the bike.

———

Andi wanted to struggle but her muscles wouldn't obey her. She knew she was in serious trouble but it was difficult to identify just what the trouble was. Her thoughts were jumbled and she couldn't focus them.

She was with André and for some reason they were walking in the river park although she couldn't remember how they had ended up there. She had lost her tote some-where along the way which was distressing because her i.d. and credit cards and the key to her condo were in it.

In the next moment she forgot about her tote. Her stomach was beginning to roil and she knew she had to throw up. She tried to swallow against the rising bile but it was no good.

"Sick." She tried to drop to her knees to puke but someone was holding her arm keeping her on her feet and she ended up puking on her sneakers and that someone's leg.

"Stupid bitch. Jeezus." The voice sounded like André's

only meaner. Her head lolled to the side. It was André. She knew André. Handsome André. Too bad he wasn't Perseus.

She wished her brain was working better. She kept losing her train of thought. The hand on her arm shook her. She wanted to pull away but fingers dug deep into her flesh. She cried out and André slapped her.

"Quiet. We don't want any company for this. I'd prefer to wait until nightfall but you are a hard woman to get alone after dark."

"Wait." She was missing something important. Something she needed to remember. Something . . .

They were near the river's bank. The grassy park gave way to large boulders that lined the river, dumped there a century before in an effort to prevent the river from eroding the land during flood stage. Andi's foot stubbed against a hard, smooth surface and she lurched forward.

"Not just yet, Andromeda. You'll slip beneath the surface soon enough. I chose this spot because it's nice and deep and the current should carry you down to the sewage treatment plant. A fitting ending I think. I usually prefer to dump my victims into the mouth of the La Crosse River and let them float down to the park for someone to find, but I don't want you found just yet."

Throwing up had helped clear some of the fog from Andi's brain but not nearly enough. She was lucid enough to know she was in grave danger but not thinking clearly enough to do anything about it.

She focused on what André was telling her. He liked to dump people in the river. *He* was the serial killer. André Lightfoot, popular soccer player, teacher of children, liked to drown his victims. And he had her at the river's edge. She was to be the next victim.

In the distance she heard the roar of a motorbike. The

sound reminded her of Perseus. Perseus had a bike. A big, black, gleaming monster of a bike with lightning bolts on the gas tank. Pretty bike. He was so handsome. And his brother was a god. She still found that hard to believe.

She'd had sex with him. At least she wouldn't die a virgin. She didn't want to die. She wanted to see Perseus again.

She tried to struggle but her muscles wouldn't obey her brain's command. She felt like a rag doll.

"No point fighting it, Andromeda. You might say I'm doing you a favor. I don't imagine being married to that pompous ass Angus Ames would be much fun for you."

"Why?" The question was little more than a whisper.

"Why? Because I can of course. I've always enjoyed a challenge–on and off the playing field. Abducting women and killing them–then getting away with it–is the ultimate challenge, don't you think? The stupid police don't even realize they have a serial killer on their hands. I'm too clever for them. It's a delicious feeling to pull the wool over their eyes, Andi. To know that I'm smarter than everyone else."

"Ashley." André had killed Ashley. Poor Ashley.

"Ah yes, your friend Ashley was only too happy to have a drink with me after your other friends left. I had hoped to get you that night but I took what was offered. She was almost too easy. That's when I knew I had to step up my game. I took you in broad daylight with witnesses. I'll tell the police I walked you home because you were a little tipsy. You must have decided to take a walk by the river after I left you. Poor Andromeda White. I'll look suitably devastated. Will your parents be gutted by their loss I wonder? We shall see."

He hooted with laughter. "Time's up, Andromeda. I'm tired of talking and the longer we stand here the more chance that someone will happen along. It's a shame really because I almost like you, but one must seize opportunity when it presents itself, wouldn't you say?"

---

Perseus parked the bike and headed down the jogging path that ran along the river. To his left was a narrow, open, grassy field shaded by huge cottonwoods and maples. To his right a border of low shrubs separated the path from the water.

He found Andi's leather tote near the path, its contents spilled. He didn't stop to take the time to pick them up. Breaking into a run he shouted her name but she didn't respond.

There was no one in the south end of the park. He almost stopped and turned toward the north but Zee was covering that end and something propelled Perseus forward. Moments later he spotted Spook's cat carrier tossed into the bushes. The kitten was crying but fear drove Perseus on. Spook would be safe enough in his carrier until he came back for him.

The shrubs grew abruptly denser and taller, blocking his view of the water although he could still smell it. He slowed and listened and thought he heard a man's voice. A moment later he spotted a break in the bushes and plowed through them. He emerged on top of a rounded boulder next to the water in time to see André Lightfoot push Andi into the river.

André turned and smiled at Perseus, then disappeared into the bushes.

Perseus let him go. His priority was saving Andi. She had sunk beneath the water's surface and hadn't reappeared.

Perseus kicked off his shoes and leaped into the river

striking out downstream. The strong current carried Andi swiftly south. He swam a few strokes and dove under to search for her, came up for air, swam a few more strokes and dove again.

On his second dive he caught a light colored flash ahead of him. He surfaced again and swam to where he thought he had seen her before diving for the third time. This time he saw Andi clearly but he was still too far away to grab hold of her. She wasn't making any effort to save herself and that frightened him.

The thought that he might be too late to save Andi spurred him on. On the fifth dive he was able to grab her and bring her to the surface. It took him several more minutes to drag her to the river bank where he could begin CPR.

How long had she been under and unable to breath? It felt like an eternity to him but had it been that long? Two minutes? Five?

Her lips were tinged with blue. Not a good sign.

"Come on Andi, breathe," he begged. Water dribbled from her mouth. Perseus whipped out his phone and called Zee while he continued to compress her chest with one hand.

"I need an ambulance. I'm at the south end." He hung up, trusting that Zee would do what needed to be done and returned his focus to the CPR.

Zee and the EMTs showed up almost simultaneously nearly ten agonizing minutes later. The emergency personnel pushed Perseus out of the way and took over.

"Will she make it?" Zee asked. He had recovered Andi's tote and Spook and handed them to Perseus. His brother looked bleak and fierce, like he wanted to throttle somebody.

The ambulance driver had parked on the grassy field near the path so the technicians were able to quickly get Andi into the ambulance. They placed an oxygen mask over her face before taking off with both the siren and flashing lights. They wouldn't let Perseus ride in the ambulance because he wasn't family.

"I need you to contact the detectives who worked Ashley's death and tell them the serial killer's name is André Lightfoot." Perseus handed back the tote and Spook. If Andi didn't make it his heart would be broken. The knowledge that he could lose her nearly paralyzed him.

"Lightfoot? Are you sure?"

"Yeah. Bastard smiled at me just before he pushed Andi into the river. Then he ran. He knew I'd save her before I'd chase him."

"I don't get it. All those years of summer camp–Andi should be a good swimmer."

"I think he drugged her. I have to get to the hospital."

Perseus turned and raced back for the bike.

THE FIRST THING Andi noticed was how awful she felt. Her head pounded. Her mouth felt like it was full of dry cotton and her stomach cramped. Something covered her face.

The second thing she noticed was the smell of antiseptic and a soft, steady beep-beep near her ear.

She took several deep breaths trying to calm her stomach and the pounding in her head. Only then did she realize that she lay in a bed and her right hand felt warm compared to the rest of her body. She shivered and opened her eyes, closing them immediately against the light.

"Andi."

The warmth moved from her hand to stroke her arm, then cradled her cheek.

"Sweetheart, open your eyes."

Perseus. She'd know his voice anywhere.

The warmth left her cheek. She wanted it back.

"Nurse, I think she's waking up."

Waking up? What in the world was going on? Andi forced her eyes open, shut them again.

"The light," she tried to whisper but the thing over her face prevented her from speaking. She began to struggle.

"Hang on Andi, it's all right. I'll get the nurse."

Nurse? She heard someone move.

"I think the lights are too bright."

"Try to open your eyes again, Miss White." This time a woman's voice, one she didn't recognize. She noticed other sounds now as well. More voices but not close by. Metal clanging against metal. The sound of something rolling.

Andi opened her eyes. A stranger leaned over her. She wanted to scream but the thing still covered her face.

"Shhh. It's all right. You're in the hospital. My name is Amelia Hart, I'm a nurse. I'm going to remove the oxygen mask now, okay?"

Andi nodded. The thing covering her face was only an oxygen mask. She tried to slow her breathing to calm her racing heart.

Nurse Hart pulled off the mask. "There. I'm going to go call the doctor. Your fiancé is right here."

Andi slowly turned her head. She wore a hospital gown and lay in a hospital bed. "What—why am I here?"

"You don't remember?" Perseus stroked her hair and grasped her hand again. She had an iv drip in the back of her left hand.

Andi tried to think back. "I went to see Pandora and Sam." Her voice cracked and broke.

Perseus slipped a straw between her lips and she drank thankfully. The water felt wonderful on her raw tongue. She held it in her mouth for a few blissful moments before swallowing.

She went to see Pandora and Sam. Then she walked home. She let her eyes roam over the white walls while she wracked her brain.

No. She didn't walk home. She ran into André and he talked her into having a drink at Sloppy's. Her gaze returned to Perseus. The nurse had called him her fiancé but that couldn't be right.

"I can't remember. I had a drink with André."

Perseus's hand tightened on hers. He had come so close to losing her. If he'd arrived even a few seconds later he wouldn't have seen her go into the water. A few seconds later and she would have drowned.

Even so, it had been touch and go for a while. The doctor had told Perseus that his use of CPR and the quick arrival of the EMTs had saved Andi's life. He felt tears come to his eyes and let them fall.

Andi reached up and wiped the wet from Perseus's cheek. "Tell me."

So he told her. The state police had stopped André on the interstate, headed east. They had found the date rape drug in her urine and more in his bags. Even if Andi never remembered what happened they had enough to charge the soccer player with attempted murder, but Detective Lee seemed to think André would need to brag about how clever he'd been and they'd get a full confession.

While Perseus spoke Andi never took her eyes from his face. She loved that face. Loved his expressive green eyes.

"Have you contacted my parents?"

"No." Perseus's gaze was steady. "They gave up their rights when they sold you to the highest bidder. You can't marry Angus Ames, Andi."

"I have to, Percy. You know I can't let all those people suffer." The urge to cry made her chest ache. Or maybe it was the after effects of the CPR.

"Listen to me. I've had a lot of time to do nothing but think. I'm a turnaround specialist, remember? I believe I can help your father save Cepheus White Sports without sacrificing you to Ames. But there's a cost."

Andi regarded him warily. "How? And what cost?"

"I've made contacts over the years. So has Zee. We're sure we can find someone to supply your father's company with the product it needs. As for the cost–you have to marry me instead."

Perseus held both her hands gently in his own. "Andromeda White, I love you with all my being. Will you make me the happiest of men and marry me?"

She knew the lump in her throat had nothing to do with the lingering effects of the date rape drug. She felt overwhelmed with her love for this wonderful man even though she'd known him only a short while. Everything about him felt right to her.

"I love you too," she whispered. "Yes, I'll marry you. But we have to–" The kiss Perseus gave her left her breathless. And wanting more. "–save Dad's company," she managed to choke out.

Perseus's eyes sparkled with devilment. "Already working on it, love. Zee and I have an appointment with your father tomorrow morning to find out exactly what he needs. We've also contacted two clothing factories that we've dealt with before. I think Angus is going to find himself scrambling for a new market to sell his goods to."

The doctor breezed into the room and put an end to their conversation. "You're a lucky woman, Miss White," he said after he had checked her vitals and eyes. He was thin and wiry, with close cropped white hair and tired brown eyes.

"If this young man hadn't come along when he did you would have been another tragic drowning. I want to keep you overnight for observation but I daresay you'll be able to leave the hospital first thing tomorrow."

# CHAPTER 26

THE WEDDING TOOK place in Italy and was the strangest affair Andi had ever attended. They were married in the side garden of Perseus's father's favorite villa, a cluster of buildings the size of a small village that housed dozens of relatives, set on a mountainside overlooking a lake so blue the color looked unreal.

There were too many guests for Andi to catch all their names. And they weren't there just for a simple, afternoon wedding ceremony–apparently family tradition dictated a week long celebration.

Gods, demigods like Perseus, and mere mortals like herself and Sam's family all mingled and partied together like equals. Andi was somewhat taken aback when she met Zee's father Zeus, but the father of the gods turned out to be incredibly charming, albeit somewhat competitive.

She soon learned that any wedding involving a god or part god demanded games of competition. Andi overheard Pandora warn Zee that he better not beat his father at *anything*–emphasis on anything–or he'd have her to deal with. To Andi's amusement Zee kissed Pandora on the nose and promised her this wasn't the year. *"But it's coming,"* he warned her as he ran off to join in the javelin throw.

What's coming?" Andi asked.

Pandora scowled at her. "If Zee ever beats his father at the games he takes Zeus's place as father of the gods. I'm not ready to deal with that."

"Holy crap."

"I know, right?" Pandora's attention snapped to her eldest daughter. "No, Mia. You cannot ride Aunt Tia's dog. Dozer isn't a horse."

Pandora wandered off to rescue Tia's lovable mutt and Perseus took her place by Andi's side. He slid an arm around her waist and pulled her close, nuzzling her ear.

"My family takes a little getting used to."

Andi pulled her head back to look at him. "You think?" She waved her hand at the scene before them. "This is a little out of the ordinary for us mere mortals."

"Would it have made a difference?"

Andi smiled and leaned against her husband. "No," she said softly. "I married you, not your family."

Perseus pursed his lips. "Wellll, actually when you marry one of us you do marry the whole family. It's too late to change your mind though. I'll never let you go now."

Andi kissed the strong jaw of the man she loved more than life itself. Perseus had not only saved her life he had also rescued her father's company. As he had threatened, Angus Ames had cancelled his contract with Cepheus White Sports when Andi told him she wouldn't marry him.

Perseus and Zee had filled the void with only two weeks of idle time for the sports memorabilia company, two weeks that turned into paid vacation for the employees, something that Cepheus had decided to make a new tradition. Things at Cepheus White Sports were back on track.

Andi had given her notice and no longer worked on spreadsheets all day. After a long discussion with her father he had reluctantly agreed to not interfere in her quest for work that better suited her.

When they returned to the States Andi planned to set up a daycare center geared for underprivileged children with a focus on art and sports. Pandora had signed on as her first investor. Lauren had agreed to teach yoga classes geared for kids. Sam's oldest boy Luke had signed on as their whiffle ball coach.

André Lightfoot sat in a cell awaiting trial with no hope of parole–ever. It wouldn't bring Ashley or any of his other victims back, but his arrest helped the victims' families gain closure.

As for Andi's own family, it would take time to heal the wounds. Meanwhile she had Perseus and a large clan of interesting characters who accepted and liked her for who she was–plain old Andromeda White.

---

I'm glad you found this book out of the millions available. If you'd like to know when I release a new book instead of leaving it to chance you can sign up for my newsletter. You can also see what I'm working on or even send me an email–all through my website, CharleyMarshBooks.

---

Turn the page for a preview of *Artemis*, another book in the Romancing a God series.

# ARTEMIS

Tia Smith strode through the double etched-glass doors of
Orion Development and scowled. Her first visit to the
company her father had insisted she work with on the
bayside project and she already hated them. In her opinion, a
company who paid to have the constellation Orion etched
into dark smoked glass along with their name in fancy script
was a company who overcharged their clients.

Tia was fiercely protective of the people affected by her
projects, and Bayside Commons was the largest project her
young company had put together to date. The scope of the
project would provide lots of opportunity for unscrupulous
firms to pad costs and skim off the extra.

She was determined not to let that happen with Bayside.
She'd worked too hard setting the project up to let some
arrogant businessman scupper it for her.

She paused just inside the glass doors and eyed the large,
luxurious reception area. A half dozen brown leather club
chairs ranged in cozy seating groups against one wood
paneled wall to her right. Real wood paneling, she noted. Not
that fake veneer crap that was all the rage in the last century.

The chairs were fronted by several glass coffee tables and faced a wall of windows looking out over Portland's harbor and working waterfront.

She smelled coffee, rich leather, and the faint briny smell of sea water that told her Orion Development believed in open windows.

Oil and watercolor paintings of Portland's early days hung on the paneled walls. A quick glance at the one closest to her told Tia they were originals by some of the city's finest artists.

The room looked like it belonged in a high class private men's club, not an office complex. It was an in your face reminder that OD was so successful they could afford to waste a windowed wall, usually reserved for high-powered executives, on their waiting room, and consequently on their clients.

It was brilliant marketing.

Tia's scowled deepened. She despised ostentatiousness in any form. In her mind, Jack Orion's company displayed it in spades. She expected the man himself to be even worse. Damn her father and his meddling.

A little research into the highly public Orion had turned up a man who played hard and went through beautiful women like they were a bottomless commodity. In his life they probably were, she thought with disgust. Orion had everything shallow, status seeking babes wanted—money, prestige and power, and looks.

She headed across the lush deep blue carpet to the only person in the room. A receptionist sat erect behind a sleek desk built from polished mahogany that held a state of the art communication system and computer. A small name plaque identified her as Ashley Hayes.

Ms. Hayes matched the room—deep blue skirt suit, red-brown hair pulled back into a snug bun, everything neat and prim and well put together, make-up expertly applied to her slightly slanted eyes and generous lips.

In contrast, Tia was dressed to visit the building site in slim jeans, a faded Rolling Stones tee-shirt, and scuffed leather boots.

The receptionist stopped tapping the keyboard with her long nails and the faint clatter that Tia had detected upon entering the Orion offices stopped.

Much to her mother's dismay, Tia kept her own nails neatly trimmed. She couldn't stand that tap-tap-tap that long nails made when working a keyboard, something she spent many hours at. That, plus the fact that Tia worked with her hands and often beat them up, meant short nails, no polish.

*"Darling, how do you expect to attract a man when you don't make the most of your feminine qualities?"* Her mother's voice echoed in Tia's head.

How many times had Tia listened to her mother's lectures on luring a man?

What her poor, well-meaning mother didn't understand was that Tia had her work. The job kept her busy, usually seven days a week. So far she hadn't met any men who were more interesting than her job.

The receptionist smiled with her deep red lips–lips that exactly matched her nails–a smile that did not reach her dark brown eyes. Tia wondered if the woman always coordinated her lips and nails. Why would a person do that? Didn't the woman have better things to do with her time?

"Welcome to Orion Development. How may I help you?"

The woman's voice was smooth and cool. Obviously she didn't understand the meaning of the word "welcome" as there was none in her tone.

"Tia Smith. I have an appointment with Jack Orion," Tia answered.

The receptionist clicked a few keys. "I see you are scheduled to meet with Mr. Orion at ten o'clock."

"I just said that, didn't I? Let him know I'm here, please."

The receptionist's eyes grew even frostier. She turned away from Tia and tapped her headset. She spoke softly into it, then turned back to Tia.

"Mr. Orion will see you now," she said curtly as she rose from her desk. Even in sky high heels she barely came to Tia's shoulder. Wordlessly she walked to the back wall and opened a cleverly camouflaged door. She stepped into the office ahead of Tia.

Jack Orion's office had polished oak floors mostly covered by a large, blue Persian rug. The rug was old, the blue color far rarer than the more common red rugs. Tia's practiced eye could see that it had been well made, likely with several hundred knots per inch.

Floor to ceiling windows filled the wall to Tia's left with a leather sofa and two facing leather chairs attractively arranged in front of it. Shelves filled with books and models of buildings and ships lined the opposite wall. She had to admit that she liked the room, despite the fact that she was prepared not to like the room's occupant.

Tia's gaze rested on Jack Orion, seated behind a modern, black, U-shaped console holding three computers. He had yet to look up from the screen he was watching. "I'll be with you in a sec."

His voice was deep and smooth and softer than Tia had expected. She wondered if he sang. He had a great voice for it.

"Mr. Orion, Ms. Smith to see you." The receptionist hesitated, stepped closer to the desk. Her voice softened. "Can I get you anything, Jack? Coffee?" she asked.

"Not at the moment, Ashley. I'll let you know."

Tia watched them with detached curiosity. She found that observing the dynamics between people proved useful in her business dealings. The way a boss treated an employee told her a lot about the boss. Was he courteous? Patient? Or rude and demanding? Was the employee respectful? Over-familiar? Cowed?

It was obvious to Tia that the receptionist was definitely sweet on Jack Orion, but he had barely looked at her. He either didn't want to show any hint of romance in front of a stranger or he wasn't interested in Ashley.

The receptionist gave Tia another cold look and left the office, leaving the door open, most likely so she could eavesdrop on Tia's meeting with her boss.

Tia stepped over and closed the office door firmly behind Ashley, then moved to stand in front of the desk. This was a private meeting. She had a few things to set straight with Jack Orion and she didn't want any interruptions.

The man in question rose from his desk as she crossed the room. He was tall, at least six-five, with broad shoulders that filled out his perfectly-fitted suit, a handsome face framed by dark blonde hair in need of a cut. In short, he was cut from the same god-like cloth as Tia's brothers. Too damn attractive for their own good.

Jack Orion held out his hand. Warm and dry and powerful, it nearly engulfed Tia's own.

"It's good to finally meet you, Ms. Smith. I find it hard to take the measure of a man—or woman—through email or over the phone. I prefer personal meetings myself."

Dark blue eyes studied her intently. Tia could see faint

lines radiating from their outer corners–whether from laughter or sun exposure she couldn't say.

"Why don't we move over to the windows while we talk?" he asked. "I find the activity on the docks fascinating."

He still held her hand. She gently freed herself. "Whatever you'd like, Mr. Orion," she said, cool and polite.

She had read everything she could find on Jack Orion and his company before making this appointment. Nothing she'd seen so far contradicted her findings. Handsome, athletic, and very wealthy–in essence Orion was a man used to having things his way.

The society reporters loved him. He often graced their pages with a different–always beautiful–woman at his side, attending the orchestra, museums, gallery openings, regattas. One of Portland's most eligible bachelors, Jack Orion was a big fish in the city of Portland.

She followed him to the seating area and took one of the chairs. Crossing her long legs she waited to see how he intended to address her concerns. He surprised her when he didn't dive immediately into business.

"I often nap on this couch," he said as he settled onto it. "But please don't tell my receptionist. Ashely believes I'm in here working my fingers to the bone when I tell her to hold all calls. I'd hate to have her image of me ruined." His blue eyes twinkled, inviting Tia in on his little secret.

Damn if she didn't want to smile at him. She pressed her lips together and reminded herself why she had made the trip across town to his office.

"Mr. Orion–" she began.

"Jack, please. We'll be working closely together for the next three years. Mr. Orion will be tedious to say and to hear after one week. May I call you Tia? That's what your friends call you, isn't it?"

Tia frowned. Her first meeting with Jack Orion was not going as planned. He kept derailing her.

"Call me whatever you like, Mr. Orion. "There are several points I want to clear up before we actually begin working together. I don't know how much my father told you about the Bayside Project–"

"Enough to get me interested." What her father hadn't told him was how beautiful his daughter was.

"That's what I'm afraid of. He probably told you about the office buildings and condominiums and neglected to tell you about–"

"Excuse me a moment, Tia. I think I'd like some coffee after all. Can I have Ashley bring a pot and two cups?"

Tia took a deep breath and reined in her temper. "Thank you, that would be nice." She smiled sweetly. If any of her brothers had seen that smile they'd know to run and run fast.

Five minutes later she sat with a cup of coffee balanced on her leg. She took a sip of the dark roasted brew and waited to see if the man across from her was going to come up with anything else to keep her from saying what she came to say.

Jack drank his coffee while he studied Tia Smith. She was not at all what he had expected. He was used to beautiful women. They flocked to him and enjoyed his companion-ship. He could easily place them all in a mold–beautiful features, perfect form, lovely clothes and jewels, soft and feminine. The ones he dated more than once also possessed intelligence.

He had been surprised and intrigued when he shook Tia's hand to feel callouses on her palm. Most women who looked like Tia and had the money to do whatever they wanted had soft, weak hands. Hers had felt strong and firm. The hands of someone who actually did physical labor.

He found that strangely appealing.

Her physical presence filled his office. She had to stand nearly six foot in bare feet, with a lean, athletic body and a beautiful face framed by dark–nearly black–curls. Intelligence gleamed from her moss green eyes.

Those large eyes studied him now. He set down his coffee cup and leaned back on the sofa, put his feet up on the coffee table and prepared to spar with the lovely Tia. Anticipation made his blood quicken.

"So, you have a few points you wish to clear up before we move forward."

"Yes. I do, as a matter of fact. Did my father also tell you what I have planned to help with the housing shortage for the underprivileged?"

"He may have mentioned something about that being part of the project. We didn't get into details. He wanted to leave that up to you."

Tia stopped herself from rolling her eyes. Her father had a tendency to drop his children "in the soup" as they liked to say. He found it amusing to set them up in difficult situations so he could see how they wriggled out of them.

His children, on the other hand, were seldom amused by Father's little "lessons" as he called them.

"Oh, I think you must know more about my housing plan than you're admitting, Mr. Orion," Tia said mildly. "After all, didn't you leave a threatening letter and a cooler full of rotting fish heads on my doorstep?"

---

You can find Artemis at your favorite retailer here:https:// books2read.com/u/mqrXGd

Charley Marsh's curiosity drove her to climb mountains, canoe rivers, and explore caves and wilderness areas from Maine to California. She's been shot at, caught in a desert flash flood, and almost drowned off the Maine coast. Once she tobogganed down a 5,000+ foot mountain.

Life is always an adventure if you have the right attitude.

Charley never set out to be a storyteller, but looking back on the elaborate lies she made up as a troubled teen she can see that she always had the makings. Now, in the immortal words of Lawrence Block, she happily "makes up lies for fun and profit."

If you would like information regarding Charley's new releases or simply want to contact Charley visit: https://charleymarshbooks.com/

Junkyard Dog Collection 4 Books 10-13

## UPHEAVAL SERIES

Slow Walk

Edge of Reality

Solstice Moon

Upheaval Series Collection

## ROMANCING THE GODS

Pandora

Cassandra

Artemis

Andromeda

## ROMANCE

Twisted Sister

## DESTINATION DEATH MYSTERY SERIES

Stalked in Paradise

Masked in Paradise

Frozen in Paradise

Buried in Paradise